WALKING TO THE
BUS-RIDER BLUES

2003 2004 Bluebonnet list

Harriette Gillem Robinet

WALKING TO THE BUS-RIDER BLUES

SCHOLASTIC INC.

New York   Toronto   London   Auckland   Sydney
Mexico City   New Delhi   Hong Kong   Buenos Aires

ISBN 0-439-28354-X

12 11 10 9 8 7 6 5 4 3 2   1 2 3 4 5 6/0

Printed in the U.S.A.   40

First Scholastic printing, October 2001

Book design by Angela Carlino

The text of this book is set in Janson Text.

I wish to acknowledge the kindness of people in beautiful Montgomery, Alabama. When my husband and I visited in June, 1997, they told us, "Montgomery has changed, you know." And we agreed.

However, as a writer of historical fiction for young people, I believe that if we don't know our history, we're sometimes tricked into repeating the worst of it. I also believe that unless we learn about where we're "coming from," we won't appreciate where "we are," or know where "we're heading."

And so I wrote *Walking to the Bus-Rider Blues*.

I dedicate this book to August Paul Aleksy III, proprietor; his wife, Tracy Reynolds Aleksy; and their son, August Paul Aleksy IV, of Centuries and Sleuths, a history-mystery bookstore in Oak Park, Illinois. Augie, Tracy, and AJ have been responsible for getting hundreds of my books into the hands of readers, young and old. Thank you, guys.

WALKING TO THE BUS-RIDER BLUES

CHAPTER ONE

That June afternoon the back storage room of Greendale Grocery store was hot. Dust specks danced in sunlight blazing through the doorway. June of 1956 was like none other; the very earth seemed to be crying out. I knelt opening a cardboard box of canned tomatoes. While Mr. Greendale was in the front serving someone, I was in the back worrying about money.

To get my mind off money troubles, I began to sing my bus-rider blues. My teacher said the songs I made up were good. That day I was singing about the haunting dream I had had the night before: Hundreds of colored people were walking. Only bare feet showed—men's brown feet, women's brown feet, children's brown feet. All walking, padding softly, softly.

Then boots with white toes sticking out of them started marching like a noisy army tramping, tramping toward the bare brown feet. But the brown feet kept padding softly forward. And when the two sets of feet met, they swirled and began walking together all mixed up, white and brown. Soon some of the boots disappeared; then some white feet were bare, too. I woke up from my dream sweating.

It all happened because, instead of riding the buses, colored folks had been walking up and down the hills of Montgomery, Alabama, since December 1955—over six months ago. It seemed we might be walking forever.

> *"Oh, I'm singing the bus-rider blues,*
> *The Alabamy bus-rider blues.*
> *I got me a feeling, deep down inside,*
> *It ain't never ever gonna be the same."*

Not riding the bus during this boycott had made my life hard, but riding the bus all those years had made my life horrible. We had to change the "System." But that day the bus boycott was not my main problem.

The three of us in my family had big money problems. We were my great-grandmother, Mrs. Lydia Merryfield, also called Mama Merryfield or Big Mama; my sister, Zinnia Merryfield; and her brother—me, Alfa Merryfield. What we had was a bad case of rent-money blues at the end of every month.

It was June 20. Would we have the July 1 rent money? We worked hard, and saved, but someone had been stealing from us. Every month some of our rent money disappeared. I was determined to find out who took it.

With a finger I flicked sweat off my brow. The storage room was always stuffy, even with the back door open. I switched:

> "Oh, I'm singing the rent-money blues,
> The Alabamy rent-money blues.
> I got me a feeling, deep down inside,
> It could almost always ever be the same."

Another problem: Big Mama, Mama Merryfield, was strong. "Strong as an ox," she called herself. But lately she got confused in the head. The Lord only knew how old she was. Some people reckoned she might even be ninety by now, and she was responsible for us.

My sister, Zinnia, was fifteen and in high school; I was twelve and in sixth grade; and we both wanted to stay in school. Zinnia wanted to be a teacher. With her loud mouth, she'd be a good one. I wanted not only college, but medical school. I was a scientist.

But lately I wished I could leave school and earn more money to pay that rent. I was a good worker. I stocked that grocery store better than Mr. Greendale. His piles of lettuce might roll off, but my piled heads of lettuce, four-sided pyramids, stayed just the way I put them. I don't know what Mr. Greendale had done before I began stocking his food supplies.

I was tall and could lie about my working age. But

then again, I wasn't too good at telling lies. I shook my head and sang my bus-rider blues once more.

Mr. Greendale sneaked up on me. "Whatcha singing, boy?"

"Sir?"

"I heard y'all singing in here."

"Davy Crockett," I sang, "king of the wild frontier."

"That ain't what I heard you singing. But that's good, Alfred. This boycott's changing you, boy. Y'all learning to 'put up your dukes,' so to speak."

Mr. Greendale called me Alfred. You see, my "phantom mother," a woman I don't remember, named me—her second child—Alpha. Alpha means "first." Imagine being a second child named first? And then someone, not knowing any better, spelled it Alfa. So sometimes I let folks call me Alfred instead.

"Sir?" I said, sniffing and rubbing my nose. The potatoes and turnips in that storage room smelled earthy. I liked the smells of a grocery store.

"Y'all know what 'put up your dukes' means?"

"Fighting, sir?"

"Boxing," Mr. Greendale said with a grin. Sometimes I thought he had brain damage from boxing when he was young.

"Y'all got to be ready in this life, Alfred. Put up your dukes and keep 'em up." He was a small, wiry man. Fists jabbing the air, he looked ridiculous dancing around in the heat.

"Yes, sir," I said, stacking some cans of tomatoes in a box next to lima beans. I picked up the heavy box and wobbled into the store to fill the shelves. I limped because my knee hurt.

"Now there's a case right there, Alfred," he called, shaking his finger. "That box is way too heavy, but y'all still carried it." He stood in the doorway wiping his sweaty neck with a big, dirty handkerchief.

"Yes, sir." I began filling the shelves. First, cans of tomatoes; then, cans of lima beans. My shelves had neat, straight rows of cans, labels all facing out.

"Not that dented can," said Mr. Greendale. "You keep that one for Aunt Lydia." He walked over and poked my shoulder. "Unless you dented it on purpose. Y'all didn't dent it on purpose, did you, Alfred?"

"No, sir." He had watched me carefully slit open the cardboard carton of cans, but he liked to find fault.

I had nightmares of cutting open a carton and finding paper bags of flour all slit. I would try to hide them, and the flour would cover my arms and hands. When I lifted the box, the flour would puff in my face. Mr. Greendale would yell, "Look, Alfred's white now!" I'd moan myself awake from that dream.

I never dented any cans. Maybe sometimes I dropped one when I was in a hurry, but I understood why he accused me. His faultfinding was part of the System.

If Mr. Greendale only knew. His remarks were "small beans." I had "big beans" troubles—like needing the rent money each month. Where did money disappear to in our house? And how could the scientific method help me figure that out?

Dented can in hand, I noticed a gap in the row of

peaches. Lifting the almost empty box, I went back for peaches. Mr. Greendale, by the produce now, caught me by the belt.

"Take this spinach, and a head of cabbage," he said. He added a couple of cucumbers with soft spots, two overripe tomatoes, celery, and sprouting onions. He dropped them in the box with the can of tomatoes.

"Thank you, sir."

A woman's lily-of-the-valley perfume tiptoed ahead of her into the store. She stood patting her powdered nose with a lacy, white handkerchief.

"Evans Greendale, I have an order here." She was from his wife's family, one of the Pitts, I believe. She had the pale blue eyes and knife-thin nose of the Pitts family. Around this side of Montgomery, everyone mostly knew everyone else, Negro families and white families.

"We about ready to close the store, Emily," he told her.

"Ain't closed yet. Find me these victuals, Evans."

"Now, you can't call them 'victuals,' till y'all cook them."

"I call them what I call them." She laughed. "If y'all don't treat me right, I'll go to that supermarket in town."

Mr. Greendale took her list and began filling a box with flour, sugar, cans of cherries, and lard. I could almost smell and taste those juicy cherry pies she would bake.

I refilled that row of canned cherries. Nothing worse than coming in the next morning and finding gaps on the shelves. I kept that store stocked to perfection.

Mr. Greendale pointed to me and told the lady, "I'm trying to teach that Nigra boy to stand up for himself."

"Well, the Nigras I seen, they standing up and walking, too." She laughed at her joke. "They'll be back on the buses soon. And sitting in the rear where they belong. We have to maintain White Supremacy, you know. Nigras have to stay in their place, and their place is the back of the bus."

"This boy, Alfred," said Mr. Greendale, "invited three white boys to beat him up two weeks ago."

"He probably started the fight," she said with a shrug.

"Well, of course he did," said Mr. Greendale. "Anytime a boy ask you if you just got paid, and y'all tell him yes, you asking for a beating."

I kept a grin on my face, but it was a false grin. Those three guys were out to rob my pay—part of our rent money. It was three against one. They beat me right in front of white people I knew, and no one stopped them.

Not only that, but I saw a police car slow down as it drove by. The policeman tilted his head, staring at my bloodied face looking up at him. He rode on. The white boys kept kicking me. If I had struck one of them while the policeman was watching, I would have been arrested and beaten at the police station. More of what they called the System.

The boys had cut open my lip, bruised my knee—it still hurt—and shut my eye for two days. They stole my pay, part of our rent money. When they were out of breath, I got up and ran.

Mr. Greendale rang the total on his cash register. I liked the sound of that *ding*. I eyed that heavy box of groceries. In a minute Miss Emily of the Pitts would be asking me to carry it out to her car, so I took off the grocery apron.

"He's got to have him a plan," Mr. Greendale said, handing over her change. "Today is payday, and I see his tough friends hanging on the corner just waiting to take his money again."

He did? I felt sweat pop on my face like popcorn.

"Of course," said Mr. Greendale with a sneer, "last summer and the summer before, Alfred just took the bus home. Nobody could beat him up when he took that bus straight from my store to his home in colored Sundown."

That was the honest-to-goodness truth. When I rode the Montgomery bus, I got home safe with my pay for the rent money.

However, slow-cooking anger had come to a boil for colored folks last winter. Thursday, December 1, 1955, Mrs. Rosa Parks had refused to give up her seat to a white man on the bus. When she was taken to jail, folks got stirred up. She was a fine lady, and had worked with my sister's NAACP Youth Council.

The Women's Political Council called for a one-day boycott. Now six months had passed, and we were still walking. From Monday, December 5, until now, we colored people had refused to ride the buses. The boycott had shaken people, colored and white.

I was lucky. Those three boys had only beaten me.

I began to think about Emmett Till, murdered over in Mississippi last summer when he was just two years older than me.

Now, how could I escape those three white boys?

CHAPTER TWO

It was hot that June afternoon; a still, oven-cooking heat surrounded me. I began sweeping the store, moving slow like a turtle crossing the yard. "Keep on keeping on," the turtle seemed to say.

As I swept, I waited for Miss Emily. I was learning from the turtle. I was learning from Mr. Greendale.

And I was learning from that new minister, the Reverend Martin Luther King, Jr., who talked nonviolence. Reverend King had been appointed to Dexter Avenue Baptist church, in downtown Montgomery, about a year ago. I had never heard of him before the bus boycott.

"Boy, carry these groceries for me," Miss Emily said.

"Yes, ma'am." I carried the box out the door and

lugged it toward her car. But she drove off, leaving me in her dust.

Wings fluttered a breeze in my face. Blue Boy, a pigeon I had doctored, circled me. I waved him away and stood staring after Miss Emily, balancing the heavy box on my sore knee.

"Well," called Mr. Greendale from the doorway of his store, "whatcha gonna do?"

"I can't carry it, sir," I said. Sometimes I was slow thinking, I guess. I lowered the heavy box to the ground.

"Then how you gonna get it to her house?"

Sure, this was a delivery. "May I use the wagon, sir?" I took a deep breath. "Sir, I don't rightly know where she lives."

He folded his arms. "Well, I thought you'd never ask."

She wasn't a Pitt anymore—she'd married a Logan— and she lived about five blocks away. Loading my family's small box with her large box, I pulled the grocery wagon toward her home.

After locking the store, Mr. Greendale passed me in his Ford pickup truck. "Have y'all got a plan, Alfred?" He probably meant a plan to handle the three boys waiting for me. He was right. I had to think.

"I'm making a plan, sir," I said.

"And stop looking down as y'all walk, boy. Look up like a boy called Alfa might." He drove off laughing.

Staring after him, I wondered how he knew my real name. I supposed I'd written it on the job application three years ago. Twelve, eleven, ten. I had been ten years

old when I had begun working at his grocery store—
evenings and Saturdays during school months, every day
during the summer. I had been a tall ten. I've always
looked older than my age.

Before this job, as a kid, I'd picked pecans. Off the
ground. They shake the pecan trees. But that was pen-
nies compared to Greendale Grocery.

I glanced over my shoulder. The white boys stood in
the middle of the street, watching me. I had a feeling that
they would stay there until I came back. I'd finish that
delivery all too soon. I slowed down walking, and began
to sniff the air.

By June everything bloomed in Alabama. Roses,
magnolias, mimosas, crepe myrtle in red and white and
pink. And it seemed everything that bloomed gave off a
scent of summer calm. I liked calm. My sister, Zinnia,
was a hothead, but not me.

As I dragged the grocery wagon, I tried looking up
like Mr. Greendale had said. I discovered that the blue
sky was pretty, and marbled in white clouds.

I found Miss Emily's block, but I couldn't read the
house address. All the houses were neat cottages,
painted houses, with sidewalks paved with six-sided
blocks.

Mr. Greendale's handwriting was terrible. As politely
as I could, I asked a short, fat man: "Sir, which house
does Mrs. Emily Logan live in? Please, sir?"

"Which one y'all think she live in, Nigra boy?"

"I don't know, sir."

"Why don't 'cha know?"

I stared at the piece of paper. "I can't read the numbers here, sir."

"Y'all go to school?"

"Yes, sir."

"Why?"

"Sir?"

"Ain't doing you no good, now, is it? Nothing worse than an educated nigger."

"Yes, sir."

"Are you some of them niggers causing trouble round here?"

"No, sir."

"Them troublemakers are refusing to take the bus. You ride the bus, don't 'cha, boy?"

I had to think. "Put up your dukes," Mr. Greendale had called it. "No, sir," I said, shaking my head. "I'm staying away from trouble."

The man lifted his straw hat and scratched his bald head. A woman walked out on her porch.

"What's the boy want, Elmer?" she called, folding her arms. "What's his business on this street? Should I call the police?"

I glanced at the wagon with GREENDALE GROCERY written on it. Then I looked at myself. I wore a short-sleeve white shirt, brown trousers, and brown shoes that sweat my feet in the socks. My black bow tie was still on.

"Says he's delivering to Mrs. Emily Logan."

"Then tell him to go deliver and get out of this neighborhood," she said. "We have a decent street here."

"Y'all hear her, nigger?" asked the man.

"Yes, sir." I still didn't know which house to deliver to, but I reckoned I wouldn't learn it from them.

I dragged the wagon slowly, head down now.

"*Hiss*, boy." A pretty woman beckoned from her gate.

"Ma'am?" I kept a respectful distance from that white woman. I wasn't giving any white men an excuse to kill me. Of course, Emmett Till hadn't, either.

"Can I help you, son?" She wore a big-brim straw hat and muddy gloves.

"I'm trying to deliver groceries for Mrs. Emily Logan."

"Why, sure, son." The woman leaned on her gatepost and pointed. "She lives in that house with the pink crepe myrtle by the fence."

"Thank you, ma'am."

"Ain't you one of Aunt Lydia's great-grandchildren?"

"Yes, ma'am."

"A wonderful, educated woman. We just love her. How old you reckon she is now?"

I smiled and relaxed. "Lord only knows, ma'am. She won't tell us." I felt happy thinking about my great-grandmother. It was as refreshing as ice-cold watermelon on a hot afternoon. And this lady was kind.

Glancing around, I lowered my voice. The lady could pay a price for being kind. They called kind white people "nigger-lovers," stopped speaking to them, and could ruin their lives and businesses. That was part of the System, too.

"Thank you, ma'am," I told the lady softly as I pulled the wagon back toward my delivery house. I dragged it to the back door, and rang the bell.

A man shuffled to the screen door. "Whatcha want, boy?"

"Sir, delivery for Mrs. Emily Logan, sir." Going back down the steps, I raised the box to my sore knee, then to my chest.

Up five steps, I stopped at the screen door. The man still hadn't unhooked it. "What about the other box?"

"Sir?" I glanced over my shoulder as I leaned against the house for balance. "Oh, that one's . . . that's . . ."

Think, Alfa, I told myself. This man shouldn't know that I was taking food home. He could make trouble for me and for Mr. Greendale, too, if word got out.

Years ago, my sister, Zinnia, and I used to go to a restaurant dump for food. We'd sneak over a fence at night and fill a bag with potato skins and cabbage hearts and day-old bread.

But the owner heard that poor people were taking food, and he got dogs to guard the Dumpsters. We had a hungry winter, and then I had found the job at Greendale Grocery. No, I shouldn't tell this man.

Looking at our box on the wagon, I said, "That's another lady's food, sir."

"How'd I know that?"

I pulled Mrs. Logan's address from the flap of her box where I had stuck it, and I held it out.

Through the screen door I saw movement. A colored woman in an apron was peeking out. This colored maid nodded her head and pointed to the man's back. Shrugging and holding one palm up, she made a not-so-bad sign about him. I kept my face blank.

The man still hadn't opened the screen door. We were both trapped in the System. He had to be tough; I had to be smart. Nonviolence said you should find a peaceful way out. Think, Alfa, I told myself.

"Well, sir," I said, taking a step down. "I'll just leave this heavy box down on the grass there."

"No, y'all, don't," he bellowed, opening the door. "Come in and take it all the way to the kitchen table." He pointed and I moved in.

As I turned to leave, I saw the colored maid silently clapping for me, behind the man's back, of course.

"Thank you, sir, and good-bye," I said, nodding to her.

I had "put up my dukes" as Mr. Greendale called it, but nonviolently. One problem solved, however, I knew those three white teenagers still waited for me.

CHAPTER THREE

If only I were Superman. Then I'd be strong enough to knock those three boys' heads together. I wanted to smash their grinning faces, but I couldn't.

As I walked back toward the store, I let Blue Boy light on my fingers. I put him on my shoulder, and he pecked my ear.

Last winter I had found the hurt pigeon on the road. I set his leg with toothpicks, and washed his bloody wings. From theater trash cans I took buttered popcorn to feed him. He liked to pick popcorn from my ear.

Now, as I touched his feathery head, I began to think about the fight ahead of me. What did I need to do? I carried five dollars for two weeks' pay. Stopping on the street, I dumped the money into my handkerchief—a square of torn sheet—and tied knots. I tied one end to my belt, and tucked the other end into my pants. What white boy would reach down into my pants?

I was so busy, I almost stepped on a crack in the sidewalk. Although, as a scientist I didn't believe in, "Step on a crack, break your mother's back," I was always careful. Six-sided paving blocks made walking hard. But it could be either the phantom mother or Big Mama whose back would be hurt.

Money in my pants, I loosened my shirt to cover the belt. So far, so good. I might get beaten, but I wouldn't lose my money.

For a few seconds I imagined that when the boys jumped me, Blue Boy would give a signal. And hundreds, no thousands, of birds would fly to my rescue. Their hot, feathery wings would stir the street into a tornado of dust.

The dust would make those white boys scream and wave their arms. They would be bent over covering their heads in terror. And Alfa Merryfield, future Negro doctor, would walk away smiling. But, that was a daydream, and this fight was real.

All those catchy words from the MIA—Montgomery Improvement Association—church meetings rang in my head. I remembered: "Walk the walk and talk the talk in the manner of love." "Refrain from violence of fist, tongue, or heart." "Justice, not victory." "Win them over, don't win over them."

I remembered Reverend King talking about the early Christians who had died in the Roman arenas. I had those three lions ready to eat me alive, and my arena was the street.

First of all, maybe "in the manner of love" I could "walk the walk" and look up like Mr. Greendale had said. Last time, I'd buried my head and hardly noticed their faces. The result was I got socked, kicked, and bruised.

What about "talk the talk?" I didn't even know their names. As I drew nearer, I began to tremble. To steady myself, I leaned down and adjusted our box on the wagon. A lady who bought food at Greendale's passed.

"Evening, ma'am," I called quickly, waving Blue Boy away.

"Evening, Albert. You still working?"

"No, ma'am. Yes, ma'am, I'm delivering." Hey, I was, wasn't I? I took a deep breath. Half a block away the three boys stood straddle-legged in the middle of the street. One beat his fist in his palm.

"Ma'am, could you tell me their names?" I pointed.

"Well, Alfred, there's Mamie Martin's boy John. He's the one with the reddish hair. And Herbert and Mary Cook's boy Luke—the tallest one. And Anna May's Raymond. Raymond Baker."

Raymond Baker, Luke Cook, John Martin. They were real boys after all. "Yes, ma'am. Thank you, ma'am."

I placed our box of food in the center of the wagon. Head high, I walked straight toward those lions. Walk the walk of love, I thought. Don't have to like those redneck bigots, just love them.

I was so nervous, my knees shook. I limped slower

and slower as I drew near them, and I was glad I had gone to the bathroom before I left. Most of me wanted to run, but the rest of me could hardly move. I was practically mummified. My breath came in gasps, and I was soaked in sweat, but I held my head high.

Raymond Baker. I looked him in the eyes. Luke Cook, John Martin. The boys began to stare at me. I was walking straight for them in the street.

"What y'all doing, nigger?" asked Luke Cook, stepping back.

"Mr. Luke Cook," I said, "y'all notice I'm delivering for Mr. Greendale." I turned and looked the others in the eye, too. "Mr. Raymond Baker, Mr. John Martin. Nice to know you. I'm Al. . . ." I took a deep breath. Was it time to face up to my name, too? "I'm Alfa Merryfield."

The expressions on their faces! Oh, if my sister, Zinnia, could have seen their faces! Their eyebrows were high, their jaws dropped. Luke Cook rubbed his head. They looked dumbfounded.

One Christian against three lions in the arena. Head high, I kept walking, and they parted to let me through. After all, I was still delivering a white store owner's goods, wasn't I?

I heard John Martin ask, "How'd he know my name?"

I didn't wait to hear the answer. As we said when we were playing hide-and-go-seek, I felt I was "home free." Out of the Roman arena. Behind me, the lions were roaring. "Delivery" and "Merryfield" were two of the words I heard.

I guess they hadn't known my name, either. I walked on.

A bus was coming. I glanced back. About seven white people were on it. Before December, there would have been fifty colored people riding, too. The bus slowed down, but I wouldn't take it.

> "Oh, I'm singing the bus-rider blues,
> The Alabamy bus-rider blues.
> I got me a feeling, deep down inside,
> It ain't never ever gonna be the same."

I sang softly because I remembered my "nonviolence of tongue." With a smile, I waved to that bus driver.

The Montgomery bus System was bad. We didn't blame the company or the drivers; we blamed the System. The System made you pay in the front, then get off the front of the bus and enter in the back door. Sometimes before you reached the back door, the driver would drive off with your dime or nickel.

You'd think a boy would get used to it, but I never did.

And then of course we sat in the back of the bus. White people sat in the front. They always got a seat because colored people had to get up and give them seats. Until Mrs. Rosa Parks. That's what the bus boycott was all about.

When I was almost to Sundown, I could hear the guys calling, "Kick the can. Tree is 'it.'" A game of kick the can. I hid the wagon in weeds and ran. I wanted to play really bad. My friends and I had jobs in the summer and didn't get to play often.

"Can, my can." They were all lining up. I began to zigzag, searching for a can.

"Here's Alfa," the boys began screaming.

There. I found a soup can. "My can," I called.

We lined up. Before me was a clump of weeds. Bad luck. Couldn't move to either side. Eight of us were lined up, and I was third in line. What could I do? The tree that was "it" was a block away and straight ahead. But the weeds were high.

"One. Two. Three." With a scream, we all began to run forward. Guys on either side of me kicked their cans away from the clump of weeds. I took a deep breath and kicked my can straight up in the air and over.

Running through the weeds, I found my can and kept kicking.

I kicked harder, ran faster. When someone ran across me, I almost tripped, but my can flew toward that tree.

I splashed through one red puddle, then another. When I kicked my can on the side, it zagged crooked. I cut across Robbie, and we both fell laughing. We rolled and ran for our cans. That field was full of us in the brick-red Alabama dirt, screaming and kicking our cans.

In the first game, I came in second. In the next game, "it" was a brick wall, and I came in first. After that we must have run back and forth for half a dozen games. Then I had to leave.

I was afraid Zinnia would be angry because I was

late and because my shirt and pants were covered with red dirt. I trotted fast pulling that wagon.

At the end of our street, I saw Zinnia pacing the board over the watery ditch by our house. She was home from working at the dry cleaners, but she wasn't busy inside. Trouble, I thought as I rubbed my forehead.

"Where's Mama Merryfield?" I called.

"Not home yet. You got food?" Zinnia wore a blue flowered dress, sleeveless, with a low neck for the heat. She tore through that food box. "I got water boiling," she said.

I followed Zinnia into the house and back to our wood-burning stove. Collecting wood was another of my chores. Most of our neighbors had gas stoves.

I cut the onions and pulled out the mushy parts. Zinnia sliced cabbage. I added the can of tomatoes. We saved the cucumber and fresh tomatoes for salad. Since we often cooked together evenings, we were finished in five minutes. The cabbage soup would boil while we searched for Big Mama. Tired, I leaned against the house lath.

The tar-paper house we rented from Mr. Harris had two rooms, two doors, four windows. We had taped greased brown paper over the windows since there was no glass. I slept in the back cooking room; Zinnia and Mama Merryfield slept in the front. Our clothes hung from pegs on the wooden wall.

Before I ran out, I stuck my money in an onion bag and tucked it back in the wall. Zinnia watched me.

"How much now?" I asked her. I knew we missed

that five dollars the boys stole from me two weeks ago.

"Almost," she said. Sometimes we talked in few words, like the detectives we heard on neighbors' radios.

"The facts, ma'am!"

"Ten." She added, "Big job. Yellow house. Us, too."

Zinnia pranced out the room, but I stopped to reach for a flashlight I had found. It might get dark before we found Mama Merryfield.

"Dress," she said.

"Much?" We were walking down the middle of the street, holding back as we walked downhill.

"Fifty cents."

"Dance?"

"Saturday." She giggled. She wanted that dress, but we didn't have fifty cents extra yet. On Saturday nights she often went to dances. She walked beside me with her head high.

Her black eyes were slanted, and her brown skin was as smooth as pressed silk. On the other hand, I had big black eyes that gave me away whenever I lied. My brown skin was scarred, and I was tall. However, no one called me "string bean" anymore. Lifting boxes had built up my muscles.

We passed a store that had water fountains outside. Immediately I knew what Zinnia would do. As soon as she spied it, she whooped loudly, "Well, what d'y'all know. Some white water and some colored water. Let me see what color the colored water is."

Some white people smiled before glancing away. Most of them frowned. I stood there feeling like a fool, but a loyal fool now. I used to walk away and wait for my sister. I didn't anymore.

"Lookee, Alfa," she called loudly. "This water ain't got no color to it. Why you think the sign read, 'Colored'?"

I grinned and shuffled my feet. Sweat ran down my neck, and I had that "tight band" feeling around my head.

Next Zinnia began slurping the water for white people. That was against the law! I wanted to glance around for a policeman, but I didn't.

When Mrs. Rosa Parks went to jail, I heard she was thirsty for hours. The fountain there was only for whites, and she wasn't allowed to drink.

Zinnia called out, "This white water don't look no different, and don't taste no different. What about that?" She glanced around, grinning.

Colored people laughed, but most of the white people glanced away. A few months ago the white people would have yelled for her to stop. They might have even called the police.

"Hey, Alfa," my friend Robbie called.

"Hay is for horses," I called back. We laughed, and he walked with us for a while.

"How y'all doing, Zinnia?" called some older boys.

All the boys knew Zinnia and liked her, but she wasn't much interested in them. Like I said, we planned to attend the colored folks' Alabama State College, up on South Jackson Street. If we could get scholarships and money, that is.

Soon a flock of teens were walking and laughing with Zinnia, and Robbie and I were trailing behind like lost puppies. Working men walking home to Sundown passed us. Colored women passed us, walking home slowly. "How y'all doing, children?"

"Fine, ma'am. Fine, sir."

None of those colored folks would take the Montgomery bus. Buses that were as empty as crumb-free cookie boxes passed us. Seventy-five percent of the people riding the buses had been colored people.

And those bus drivers used to insult our colored mothers and grandmothers. Called them "black cows," "animals," and worse names. They mistreated our Mama Merryfield, though most folks, white and colored, loved her. She didn't have a mean bone in her body. But in spite of her age, she was walking like everyone else.

Now in the distance a dark woman sat under a mimosa tree full of pink blooms. Only Big Mama would be singing and rocking back and forth like that.

"I see her," I called.

CHAPTER FOUR

Mama Merryfield was singing:

"Ain't gonna let nobody turn me around,
Turn me around, turn me around,
Gonna keep on a-walking,
Gonna keep on a-talking,
Keep on walking to the Promised Land."

They called that old church hymn a civil rights song now. Our struggle against the System was a struggle for our civil rights. Due to this boycott, Montgomery was shaken like a hayfield in a hurricane. The buses were empty and so were the stores downtown. Business was suffering, and so were we.

A "great and glorious struggle for freedom," the Reverend King called it. Yet nobody knew if it would be successful.

And an old colored lady, our Big Mama, was left sitting on the street. Her tan blouse hung outside her brown skirt. A black-straw pillbox hat sat on gray braids twisted in orderly rows. When she had ridden the bus, she had arrived home every evening. Now, walking, she sometimes got lost.

I ran and reached her first. "Big Mama," I called.

"I knew you children would come find your Big Mama," she said. She glanced all around me.

"What happened, Big Mama?" asked Zinnia, running up. "You should be 'shamed of yourself, sitting here."

I winced. In the last year it was as if Zinnia were the mother, and Big Mama were the child.

Mama Merryfield moaned and rubbed her bare feet. "You children don't know," she said, and she stared at Zinnia.

My sister knelt on one side of her and I knelt on the other. Robbie said, "See yuh," and left. Some of the boys stood, hands in pockets, staring at Big Mama. Zinnia and I began putting her socks and shoes back on.

Big Mama's feet were large and lumpy. Every joint had a bony knob called a bunion. She wore men's shoes we found in trash cans, and she cut holes for her bunions. That day her shoes were yellow leather boots. I shoved her foot into one of them.

"Alfa, is that you?"

"Yes, Big Mama."

"Where's Zinnia?"

"She's right there, Mama."

"'Course she is. Was I on the right street?"

"Big Mama," Zinnia said, "here I am fixing your feet to walk, and you ask, 'Where's Zinnia?' Are you blind, too?"

I rubbed my forehead. Couldn't Zinnia see Mama Merryfield was confused? "We'll walk you home, Big Mama."

"Oh, thank you, son. Zinnia, who is this nice young man?"

I saw the boys back up. "It's okay," I told them. "She's tired, that's all."

We pulled her to her feet. "Ah, that's good," she said. "That little rest helped my feet."

Standing, Mama Merryfield seemed powerful. She was six feet six inches tall. Head high, she walked with arms swinging and her bag on her back.

Behind us, the boys began talking. "Wouldn't be no shame if she took the bus," said one.

"Where's the taxicabs supposed to be helping old ladies?"

"Yeah, why is she walking?"

Mama Merryfield swung around. "Why am I walking?" she asked, hands on hips. "Why? For my dignity, that's why. All my life it's been, 'Aunt Lydia do more here, Aunt Lydia you doing wrong there,' and they treat me like dung balls.

"Dignity!" She stopped. "You know how dignity feels?"

The guys stood, hands in and out of pockets, and stared up at Mama Merryfield. She towered over them like a mighty magnolia tree.

"Dignity," she called. She thumped her chest. "Now I know how dignity feels."

She began walking in the wrong direction. I grabbed her elbow and turned her around. A bus headed for Sundown passed, empty except for the driver. He stared at us.

"Mama Merryfield, no wonder you don't come home," Zinnia said. "You don't even know which way to walk. Are you out of your mind? We sick and tired of looking for you."

Big Mama's lips pressed together, and she walked faster. Her nostrils flared, and her eyes, now gray with age, stared ahead. I noticed how high she held her head, her and Zinnia, too.

We not only reached home quickly, but the cabbage soup was perfect, and our cucumber-tomato salad delicious.

The next night Mama Merryfield arrived home in time to go to the MIA's meeting. Big Mama and I walked to the Holt Street Baptist Church in forty-five minutes; Zinnia stayed home. As soon as folks saw Big Mama, they called: "Mama Merryfield, ma'am, y'all come on in here and sit down, ma'am." They walked her inside, and the crowd closed behind her. The meetings began at seven o'clock, but I heard that by five o'clock the church was packed fuller than a bag full of mothballs.

Outside, I wormed myself through the crowds of people to reach an open window. Although there were loudspeakers, other people—men, women, children—were standing under church windows to hear too. I crept to sit on the grass with my back to the redbrick wall.

After the usual prayers and a hymn, some man reported on talks with the bus company and the city. "They still telling us no," he said. "We only got three demands: First, we want to sit down, first come, first served. Colored folks starting from the back. White folks starting from the front. Second, we don't want to give up no seat to a white person."

People clapped and cheered.

"And, third," he said, "we want some colored drivers on our routes."

Next, I heard someone tell about the court cases. I couldn't see him, but he said, "Our lawyers appealed to the federal district court. They said all bus segregation is unconstitutional."

People clapped and called, "Amen!"

"But," he said, quieting them, "Mayor Gayle said, 'We must maintain White Supremacy.' He and our Montgomery commissioners won't take no court case sitting down." Sitting down? Inside the church, people laughed. Outside, where I sat, folks poked each other and laughed. I laughed too.

"The commissioners have appealed to the Supreme Court."

I knew what that meant. If the Supreme Court agreed with the federal district court, our boycott could end bus segregation in the whole United States. The whole United States!

The man asked: "Do y'all want to keep walking?"

The church crowd shouted, "Yes! Amen! We gonna keep on keeping on!"

Just sitting there against the church, I felt goose bumps on my arms. Shouts filled the summer air, and you could slice the hope like juicy peaches.

Next I recognized Reverend Abernathy's voice. He had people laughing about themselves limping down those roads. The hymn "Woke Up This Morning With My Mind Stayed on Freedom" was sung with such feeling, I felt like rising on wings like a bird.

Then the Reverend King said, "Tonight we here are singing freedom songs for the same reason that our fore-parents as slaves sang them." My throat grew tight.

He told about colored people's history in America. "For two hundred years," he said, "without wages, black people, who arrived in chains—remember—drained the swamps, built the homes, made cotton king, and helped lift this nation from a colony to a world power."

That made me feel proud. He said, "Especially in the South, the hard, the dirty, the dangerous work was done by colored people." His voice was deep and soaring. It rose and fell like ocean waves. As they listened, no one moved outside. "Justice delayed," he said, "is justice denied. And there's a point where caution becomes cowardice." I loved when he said things like that.

He warned against hate. He told us that Tuskegee Institute's Booker T. Washington had said, "Let no man pull you so low as to make you hate him." I felt glad I had treated those white boys decent.

Reverend King said, "Nonviolence is a Soul force. It can redeem the nation and win first-class citizenship for all."

When he said that if you follow the rule of "an eye for an eye and a tooth for a tooth," you end up with everyone blind and toothless, people roared with laughter. Folks ended with a prayer and the hymn "Gonna keep on a-walking, keep on a-talking, keep on walking to the Promised Land."

Wiping my eyes, I stood to find Mama Merryfield. I was glad about the meeting. We were going to win. I felt it. I wished I felt as good about the rent money.

June evenings were long on light, and long on delicious smells in Sundown. About twenty houses, ten on each side, made up our block on the street. Some people grew vegetables and raised chickens in their yards. The next evening the house on one side smelled of roasted chicken; the house on the other side smelled of roasted corn.

Robbie walked by. "Hey, Robbie," I said.

"Hay is for horses," he said. We talked about school for a while. He ran off and came back with some other boys, calling, "Kick the can." I played, but not for long. Zinnia and I had to go out back and count the rent money.

As I limped in, I wished we could use a bank like well-to-do folks. Then our money couldn't disappear.

But we never had enough money to open a bank account. We never got that far ahead. Sitting in the back doorway, Zinnia and I counted the bills and change.

Mama Merryfield had come home with some extra pay that Zinnia added. "Wait," Zinnia said, going over the quarters and dimes again. "Alfa," she said, "we got the rent money."

I laughed and leaned back so fast, I bumped my head. Holding where it hurt, I said, "Way to go!"

But would the rent money disappear as it had before?

CHAPTER FIVE

Mama Merryfield resumed rocking in the front room. Zinnia glanced at me. "Big Mama," she called, "did you hear?"

I knew Big Mama had been listening because she had stopped rocking. All our lives she had counted money for the rent, but in the past year we had had to do it ourselves.

"'Course I heard. I'm old, but I ain't deaf, you know. We got the yellow house to clean. You children gonna help me."

"You didn't hear me, then," said Zinnia. "I said we have the rent money already, eight days before the first of the month."

Big Mama grunted.

She had been reading her Bible in sunlight from the

doorway. Those last rays of the setting sun lit up a photograph of her husband, the Reverend Marcus Merryfield. In an oval wooden frame, the photo swung from a nail in a lath of the wall.

His sad eyes stared out the doorway. I heard that he had been a wonderful preacher. Because he had been even taller than Big Mama was, they were called "the Gentle Christian Giants." I was going to be tall, too.

But tall Great-grandfather Marcus had died of lockjaw. Carrying his shoes in a flood, he had stepped on a nail and was dead in a short time. A horrible death, stiffened from toes, to legs, to arms, to a stopped heart. After his death, Mama Merryfield raised their two daughters and son by herself. Her gems, she called them.

Her girls were named Ruby and Pearl which isn't too bad, but her boy was named Diamond. My grandfather was Diamond Merryfield. That's a worse name than Alfa.

To make a long story short, when he grew up, Diamond moved away to New York City, married, and had ten children. One of them was a woman named Susan Merryfield. One morning, Big Mama answered a knock on her door.

Susan Merryfield had my sister, Zinnia, who was three and a half, by the hand and me in her arms. I was about six months old. This mother of ours left a suitcase of baby clothes and our birth certificates. She said she was going to the store to get milk for me, but she never reappeared. That's why I call her the "phantom mother."

Mama Merryfield lived in a better house long ago. But Ruby and Pearl were sick, and left her poorer because, when they died, she payed their bills. To help her, Mama Merryfield only had her beloved Diamond, who lived far away and had a big family. Before he had the ten children, he had sent money home. Afterward, he didn't.

So, after we arrived as babies, we ended up in this tar-paper house. Big Mama could have lived better, but Zinnia had pneumonia twice, and I had broken a leg and an arm. And there we were still, sitting in the doorway of the two-room house, holding the rent money for July 1. What a relief. "Way to go!" I told Zinnia again.

But Zinnia looked at me and rolled her eyes. I nod-ded. Other times we had celebrated having the rent money, and when we went to check it later, part was gone. We had begged and borrowed to keep from being thrown out.

Our rent was fifty dollars a month, due on the first. At ten dollars a week cleaning different houses—some-times only six or seven dollars if the white ladies were mean—Mama Merryfield only made about forty dollars a month. Mr. Greendale paid me five dollars every two weeks. That was ten dollars a month. Zinnia made about the same. Sometimes she got a tip. So our total family in-come was about sixty dollars a month, and we paid fifty dollars in rent.

In the past it had been easier to pay the rent, and we had sometimes saved some money, too. Lately we were always short. We hid the money, but there were no locks on the doors. Over my shoulder, I watched as Zinnia stuck the money in a new spot.

When I walked back into the house, Big Mama had closed her eyes. She was humming some church music. I went to bed and fell asleep to her humming.

That night I dreamed that the house burned up. Our tar-paper house was in flames, and our rent money burned up, too. I was crying because we couldn't pay the rent, and Zinnia said, "Pay the rent for what?" We had laughed.

In spite of that dream, I slept soundly. In the morning Big Mama rose early to prepare to clean the yellow house. Zinnia and I were going to work there, too. Zinnia had time off from pressing clothes at the dry cleaners, and I had the morning off. Greendale Grocery would be a mess by the time I returned.

I was standing out front when Zinnia went back to check the rent money. I heard her cry out.

"What?" I called, running into the house.

She pointed. "Someone's been in it."

"How can you tell?"

"I know how I left it."

"Count it," I said as she dumped it on her bed.

"It's short about ten dollars. Somebody took our rent money." She glanced at me, then she stared at Big Mama.

"Big Mama," I asked, "who could have done that?"

Big Mama was rolling her maid uniform and white tennis shoes and packing them in her sack. Slinging it on her back, she said, "We'll make plenty money. We got the yellow house to clean."

I looked at Zinnia. She had her hands on her hips. And I knew what she was thinking.

We had to solve this missing money problem. The best way, I thought, was to use the scientific method. Observation: Bag of money moved. Hypothesis: Big Mama moves the bag and takes the money. Evidence: She was the only one who wasn't upset that the money was missing. How could I test my hypothesis?

We followed Big Mama out the door for the long walk to the yellow house.

Dr. and Mrs. Williams owned the thirty-room, two-story, yellow house that we were to clean. It was on a hillside with a U-shape driveway. In front, six white columns stood guard from porch floor to house roof. These columns had curly parts at the top and were ridged up and down. The house was a Southern mansion.

The hillside where it stood wasn't an ordinary one. It had fancy trees with metal labels nailed on the sides. Instead of being from Alabama, these trees came from all over the world: China, Japan, Africa, Brazil. And I think the Williamses actually paid money for them. Mrs. Williams was a plant and tree lover.

In the kitchen, Mama Merryfield gave out buckets and rags. I was assigned to inside windows. A man with ladders had washed the outside. As I started to work, I spied something on a shelf.

There was a silver money clip with greenbacks in it. I noticed a hundred-dollar bill folded on the outside. My spine tingled. I had never seen a hundred-dollar bill so, holding my breath, I stood on my toes and kind of peeked at it.

I thought it was strange that Dr. Williams had left a

money clip on a kitchen shelf. The whole time I washed windows in the kitchen, that money made me feel creepy. The clip had SLW engraved on it, for Silas L. Williams. And there was a design of a stick with wings and two snakes wound around it.

While I washed other windows in the house, however, it was not the hundred-dollar bill but other money that I thought about. I kept wondering where our rent money went. Zinnia hadn't taken it, I knew, though I used to suspect her. Once when she wore a new dress to a dance on Saturday night, I asked her. But she swore she and her girlfriend had traded dresses.

I think she suspected me, too. I loved books, and my teachers lent me biology books to read during the summer. Colored students never went to the public library. Did Zinnia think I bought those books?

As sweat poured down my face, I washed those windows as fast as a speeding freight train. The smell of vinegar filled the air as I rinsed the windows, and I polished them to a shine. I had lots of good terry-cloth rags to use. The outsides of the windows were well washed; and when I finished, those windows were shining inside and out.

Mrs. Williams walked through to check on me. She tilted her head, searching for smudges, but she couldn't find any. On a return trip she sighed and said, "You're mighty slow, Alfa, now aren't you?"

"Yes, ma'am."

CHAPTER SIX

From time to time Mama Merryfield got special jobs at the yellow house. Dr. Williams was a cousin of the chief of police's father, and Big Mama had saved the father's life, carrying him to the hospital on her back when he had a heart attack.

While I washed windows that hot morning, Big Mama and Zinnia washed white woodwork, including doorways and a curved staircase, from the front entrance to the second floor. They could get by with a scrub and rub, a swipe and wipe, but I had to polish glass to a shine.

On the second floor I used my right arm and then my left. Soon both shoulders ached.

But, still, I thought about the missing money. What would Big Mama do with the money? Hide it somewhere?

If she did take it, how could I prove it? I needed evidence. Maybe I could put some wet ink on the bag? Then I would look at all our hands in the morning. But would the ink stay wet?

The last window in the attic got only a swipe of vinegar. I mean, who would notice smudges on windows in the attic?

We all finished at about the same time.

When we arrived in the kitchen, that money clip was gone. The regular maid, Mrs. Louise Cook, took my rags and buckets. "You kids," she said, "take these." She had made tuna fish salad sandwiches with lettuce, tomato, and mayonnaise. She handed us the sandwiches wrapped in waxed paper.

"Thank you, ma'am," I whispered. She made us use separate downstairs bathrooms to hide in and eat. She fed Big Mama, too; and we drank lemonade, tart and sweet, with seeds floating.

After eating, Zinnia and I went outside and sat on the back porch steps with Big Mama. We had to wait for our pay. Big Mama had changed from her uniform of black dress with white apron to her green blouse and flowered skirt.

"Y'all did yourselves proud," she told us. "We cleaned up that yellow house like greased lightning." When she hugged us, the whole world sang in my ears. It was like old times sitting on the back steps that hot afternoon. Since our pay would be rent money for July, I felt happy.

Mrs. Williams drove by us, leaving in her car. I refused

to feel angry because she was making us wait for our pay. Instead, I leaned my head against a step and breathed in Alabama's summer sweetness. A jackhammer woodpecker tattooed a tree trunk loudly, while gray and white mockingbirds protested against the noise.

Yellow sunshine and tree-leaf shadows danced across my closed eyelids. I thought about our lives. I had never walked so much in my life.

"Ain't taking no more insults from bus drivers," Big Mama said suddenly. "Or walking to the back to get on. You don't know how many dimes I payed in the front, and the driver never gave me time to even reach the back door."

Bus money, I thought. We should have had even more money because we weren't riding the buses. Where was that money going?

Observation: Money always disappeared in the night. Action: I should stay awake one night. I'd tell Zinnia to, too.

Big Mama moaned. "Stole my hard-earned money. We gonna turn them around if it takes forever and a day."

I nodded. Six and a half months from December's cold to June's heat. It just might take forever and a day, and it did make our lives hard. I was going to be awfully tired walking home that night from Greendale Grocery, and I was only twelve. I could imagine how tired Mama Merryfield felt.

"You children are my hope," Big Mama said softly. "Learn your lessons, and get yourselves some scholarships to college. That's possible."

Zinnia and I nodded.

"I remember," said Big Mama, "the day you children arrived twelve years ago by the Lord's count. I was ready to go to my eternal rest. But I said, 'These children gonna keep Mama Merryfield alive.'

"Them white social workers were scared to come. They sent a colored 'aide' to Sundown. She wanted to put you children with people my husband wouldn't have approved of. I had to show them that I could take care of you."

She shook her head. "Seems we been sinking lower every year. But, a 'bruised reed he shall not break, and a smoldering wick he shall not quench.' 'The Lord will free our feet from the snare.'"

I really hoped so.

"Big Mama, what was our mama like?" Zinnia asked.

Zinnia was always wondering about our mother. She felt Mama Merryfield was holding something back, that she wasn't telling us everything. I told her that our mama dumped us and cut out forever. If Big Mama knew where our mama was, she could get us help with that rent money.

It was always the rent money that we needed. People from church passed us clothes, even shoes. I brought home food. But the biggest chunk of money went for that monthly rent.

I glanced at Mama Merryfield. Her lips were pressed together, and she frowned. She never answered us about our mother. I wished Zinnia hadn't brought it up.

"You being raised in a Christian home with proper

manners," said Big Mama. "Ain't no sin to us being poor, as long as we're honest. And Lord knows, we're honest-to-God-poor."

Again, she didn't tell us about our mother, but it was good to have Big Mama's mind clear. I was glad Mrs. Williams made us wait. Maybe she had gone to the bank?

Zinnia said with a grin, "Y'all heard that they ain't letting us buy vanilla ice cream no more?"

I shook my head, sure it was a joke.

"Vanilla's being saved for white folks, and colored folks gotta eat chocolate." We laughed, and Big Mama hugged us.

Half an hour later Mrs. Williams drove up, followed by a policeman in his patrol car. The officer jumped out and drew his gun on us. "Get into the house," he said.

I stared at his familiar face. He was the officer who had watched the white boys beat me up.

Mama Merryfield trembled like an old person with palsy. I had to help her stand. Zinnia and I carried her by the elbows into the kitchen. Mrs. Louise Cook, the Williamses' maid, frowned and shook her head as we stumbled through the door.

On command, we lined up, the three of us and Mrs. Cook.

"Now," asked the policeman, "which one of y'all Negro radicals stole this fine family's money?"

I felt as if the atom bomb had exploded in that kitchen. I saw a flash of light and a mushroom cloud of doom. What would Mr. Greendale think? But, wait, we hadn't stolen anything. I began shaking my head no and holding my hands out palms up.

"Mrs. Williams," Zinnia said, "we haven't stolen anything from you. We just waiting for our pay for working. Just our honest pay is all we want."

I was still shaking my head no.

The policeman twirled his revolver. "Y'all better come up with the money our fine Mrs. Williams lost."

My brain was a blank. I was pleased that Zinnia had spoken up, because I couldn't think of a thing to say.

Mrs. Louise Cook said, "Mrs. Williams, have y'all searched for y'all money? None of these people here done taken it." She added quickly, "Me neither, Mrs. Williams, you know that."

Mrs. Williams turned to the policeman. "Well, ain't cha gonna search them?"

He looked aside, and his voice grew more gruff. "If I don't see that money clip and two thousand dollars on this table, I'll search every one of you."

Two thousand dollars? Who would lay two thousand dollars on a kitchen shelf? Two thousand dollars? I couldn't even imagine that much cash.

I felt angry, but even so I began making observations, reading other people's feelings. It seemed that that policeman didn't feel comfortable taking Mrs. Williams's orders. But, of course, Dr. Williams was kin to the police chief's father.

Mama Merryfield pointed to the officer. Before she even began speaking, I watched red rise along his neck and ears, and cover his face.

"Ain't you little Jimmy Newton?" she asked. "When that doctor didn't come, didn't I pull you feetfirst out of Mrs. Geraldine Newton's womb? And you so weak and puny, I nursed you for six months of my life beside my own daughter Pearl!"

Now his face was flaming red. Sunlight from the window in back lit his ears. First he patted his face with a handkerchief, then he stepped forward with hand outstretched. "Yes, ma'am, Aunt Lydia, my mama still talks about you."

With a scowl, he stepped back. "But right now I want you folks to search each other."

Search each other? How do you search each other? I pulled my shirt out. I pulled my pockets inside out and put my junk—a pencil, handkerchief, two dimes for bus fare I never used, string, red rubber bands, and my school cards—on the floor.

When I glanced up, I saw the funniest expression on Mrs. Williams's face. The policeman had his white linen handkerchief over his eyes. On the other side of Big Mama, Zinnia gurgled.

Turning, I saw Big Mama drop her skirt, petticoat, and blouse on the shiny tile floor. She stood there in her underwear. "You want to search Mama Merryfield? Well, here I am." Big Mama was pulling down her underpants.

CHAPTER SEVEN

Mama Merryfield taking off her clothes before white people! She must really be angry. The accusation made me angry, too, but she had loved that policeman as a baby, giving him some of her own child's milk. Why didn't he believe us?

The loudest moment of screaming silence I had ever heard blared forth. I thought I heard our church choir shouting for her. Angels with black fuzzy hair seemed to be climbing up and down Jacob's ladder beside tall Mama Merryfield.

I wrestled to keep her underpants up.

"You can put your clothes back on, Aunt Lydia," said Mrs. Williams with a gasp. Hand to face, she looked away.

"No, ma'am," Big Mama said, throwing her pillbox hat down. "You go ahead and search Mama Merryfield." Zinnia reached for her petticoat, and I snatched up her blouse and flowered skirt. As Big Mama stood there, Zinnia lowered her petticoat, and I pulled her arms through the sleeves of her blouse. As I snapped her skirt, I spied something that made my heart stop.

There was something in Big Mama's shoes. Greenish paper folded small. She hadn't taken off her shoes. What was she hiding? Our Big Mama was not a thief, but she could act crazy sometimes. My heart ached.

Officer Newton recovered and scowled. "Y'all Nigra radicals letting out-of-town folks get you all riled up. Not riding our buses. Not shopping downtown. Alabama had good racial harmony all these years. Now y'all Nigras saying y'all ain't been happy."

Was this why Mrs. Williams was accusing us? White people were angry about our boycott. I knew they were arresting colored drivers. But us?

After ranting and raging at us, Officer Newton seemed to remember the robbery. "Stealing from fine white families. Mrs. Williams, shall I take these people down to the station?" he asked.

He had no reason to blame us. Of course, in Alabama police didn't need a reason to arrest colored people. And police stations were dangerous. Beatings were sometimes deadly, especially for a colored boy like me. I caught my breath and felt hair rise along my scalp.

I thought of Emmett Till dying last summer in

Mississippi. Had the boycott come to this point, that they accused innocent people of crime?

Mrs. Williams waved her hand. "I'm disgusted with this show. Officer—"

Just as she was about to say something else, the screen door slammed, and Dr. Williams walked in. Mrs. Williams ran to him and wept hysterically on his shoulder. "Silas, sweetheart, it's been so horrible. They stole y'all money." She pointed to us.

I kept shaking my head no. But my mind was thinking: Why had Mrs. Williams called the police before she told her husband about it? Did she hope to find the money before he came home?

And how could we be accused of stealing? As Mama Merryfield said, we were honest-to-goodness poor, and proud of it.

At the store, Mr. Greendale sometimes gave me the day's money in a bag to take to the bank. That's how much he trusted me. And we often cleaned homes when families were on vacation. That's how much they trusted us.

Dr. Williams patted his wife's back. "Why don't we let them go home, sweetheart. We'll search the house. We've never had anything stolen before."

"I've looked everywhere, Silas darling," she sobbed, pointing. "Y'all money was right there this morning."

"Here in the kitchen?" asked Officer Newton. He frowned, then raised his eyebrows. "Two thousand dollars?"

Looking over his wife's shoulder, Dr. Williams said,

"I took it in hundreds to pay . . . the plumber. At the office. I just came back for it."

"But the kitchen?" asked the officer.

"I set it there when I washed my hands to eat breakfast." Dr. Williams glanced toward the shelf. "We can trust our colored help," he said. "We've never had any trouble."

Who pays a plumber two thousand dollars, I wondered? Why the silver money clip? That sounded strange to me. Where had that money gone?

Staring at Dr. Williams's face, I saw embarrassment. He glanced from side to side past his weeping wife. It seemed to me they weren't in agreement about losing the money, or about calling the police, either.

But we Merryfields were still accused. I began to tremble. If something happened to me, who would take care of Zinnia and Mama Merryfield? I was a colored boy like Emmett.

Emmett Till had been fourteen last summer when he had visited his friend's grandfather in Mississippi. He was on vacation from school in Chicago. His friend told folks that Emmett had said, "Hi, baby," to a white woman in a grocery store.

Later, that woman's husband and another man took Emmett by force from the grandfather's house. Beaten and murdered, Emmett was found weeks later in the Tallahatchie River.

By showing pictures of her son in his coffin, Emmett Till's mother had made sure no one forgot him. Newspapers everywhere printed the pictures, and colored people prayed for a change in the System. Now, maybe in Montgomery, Alabama, our struggle could help bring about that change.

Now I found my voice. "Please, Dr. Williams, we need our pay for the rent money. Mr. Harris comes by on the first, and we need this cleaning money to make up the rent."

He looked sympathetic, but Mrs. Williams swung around angrily. "Y'all not getting paid for anything. Furthermore, y'all will clean here for free till y'all have paid me my money."

The officer picked up on that. "All right, march out of here. Y'all lucky Mrs. Williams is kind enough to let you go."

Clean there until we paid back two thousand dollars? At the rate she paid, I'd be an old man before we made up that much. But I welcomed any reason to leave without going to the police station. In relief, I turned and walked toward the back door.

I remembered King's words: "He who passively accepts evil is as much involved in it as he who helps perpetrate it."

"Sir," I repeated to Dr. Williams, "as soon as y'all find the money, please pay us for all the work we did here this morning. We need it for the rest of our rent."

"That's a shame, a living shame," said Mrs. Louise Cook. "These folks need they rent money to pay Mr. Harris for that itty-bitty tar-paper shack in Sundown they living in."

I stopped. It hurt to hear our home called a "shack."

"If they had y'all two thousand dollars, they wouldn't need they pay."

Mrs. Williams wiped her eyes and asked, "Wait a minute, now. What did y'all say, Louise?" She put her hands on her hips and glared.

I turned to face them and walked back, although I knew it might be the most foolish act of my life. I would not walk out on Mrs. Cook. We colored had to stick together. I was going to be there for Mrs. Cook since she had had the nerve to defend us.

"I think y'all heard me, Mrs. Williams, ma'am." Hands folded at her waist, Mrs. Louise Cook stared at Dr. and Mrs. Williams. All three Merryfields had walked back to stand by her. I stood on her right; Zinnia and Big Mama stood on her left. We stood tall, looking Dr. and Mrs. Williams dead in the eyes.

Seven months ago Mrs. Cook probably wouldn't have spoken up, and if she had, she would have promptly been fired. As we all stared at the Williamses, I felt a surge of dignity.

I just hoped Mama Merryfield wouldn't do anything else crazy. Reaching across Mrs. Cook's back, I took Big Mama's warm hand. She gave my hand a squeeze.

Mrs. Williams looked at us. "Well, now what y'all think you're staring at?"

As we left, I struggled for something to say. I needed to have the last word. "I hope y'all find your money soon, ma'am," I called. "We need that rent in seven days."

• • •

The next morning my sister shook me awake by the shoulder. The air smelled clean, and felt humid against my cheek. Roosters were crowing, but the sky was jet black.

Zinnia said, "We got ourselves a problem." A cricket outside the back door chirped loudly.

Getting dressed, I joined her in taking clothes off the line and folding them. We were a feast for early-morning mosquitoes.

"A problem," I repeated. Zinnia had hit the nail on the head. It was money, not just our rent money now, the Williamses' money, too.

She said, "I was so scared you were going to jail. They couldn't mess much with me and Mama Merryfield, but they could kill you, and claim you made them do it."

"I know." I bet she wasn't half as scared as I had been.

"But now for our problem." I slapped at mosquitoes.

"Right," she said. "I read all those detective stories."

"Those are mysteries."

"Solving a problem is solving a mystery."

Zinnia read mystery stories, but I couldn't waste time on fiction. I read biographies and biology. Real stuff.

"Everyone's a suspect until proven innocent," said Zinnia.

"Whoa. Don't you have that backward? Everyone is innocent until proven guilty!"

"Hush," she said, "you'd never solve a mystery that way. Everyone's a suspect, then you look for motivation." She waved mosquitoes from her face.

Wait, I thought. I could solve problems too. Observe,

form hypothesis, collect evidence, test evidence, make conclusion. Observation: Money missing. Hypothesis: Someone stole it. Evidence: People present could have done it. But who?

I said, "Let's test to see who could have done it."

"Test?" asked Zinnia. "I just said to look for motivation."

"Mrs. Louise Cook is poor and resents years of being treated like dung balls," I said. "That's motivation."

"Ninety-nine percent of the colored people in Montgomery, Alabama, have that motivation," Zinnia said.

I imitated the police officer: "Alabama had good racial harmony all these years. Now y'all Nigra radicals saying y'all ain't been happy." I giggled. "But," I said, "we're Christian, and don't steal."

I swallowed. Once I had shoplifted a pack of yellow pencils. I had been so scared, I never used the pencils. They're still buried under the house, I guess.

"And Mrs. Cook wouldn't risk her job." I folded a shirt and smoothed it for ironing.

"But did you hear Mrs. Cook?" Zinnia said a moment later. "She said we hadn't stolen the money. Then she added, 'Me neither.' That was suspicious."

"Why are we ready to blame a colored lady?"

"You're right," said Zinnia. "I'm as bad as white folks."

I whispered, "Do you think Big Mama stole it?"

"How could you say that?" She whispered too.

"Well, she didn't take off her shoes."

"Her shoes?" asked my sister. She added quickly,

"You know she ain't dishonest, but she does some crazy things sometimes."

At that, we giggled. "Tried to take all her clothes off," I said. "I ain't never seen her bare before, not even bathing."

Since we washed up at the outside wall faucet in the neighbor's backyard, we all stayed in wet overshirts to bathe. And when it was cold in the winter, we heated water on the stove, and washed in our laundry tub.

Zinnia was still laughing silently. "Lordy, she must have been real angry to do that."

"As much pride as Mama Merryfield has, being blamed for stealing must have really hurt her feelings."

"Did she say anything about it walking home?"

"No, we never said a word. Halfway back, she sat under a tree and took off her shoes for a while. Then we finished walking. While I went to Greendale, she washed our laundry."

Zinnia and I had just about folded the clothes off the clothesline into neat piles on my cot. The clothes were ready for ironing. I took a deep breath.

My sister was a mystery-story expert, and I was a scientist. Surely between us, we could not only find out about the money missing in our house, but about the money missing from the yellow house. We had to. We needed to clear our names.

"Who else can we suspect?" I asked Zinnia.

CHAPTER EIGHT

"**Speaking** of blaming people," I said, "what do you think of Mrs. Williams?"

"Suspicious," said Zinnia. "Either she needed to find her husband's money before he came home. Or she stole it and blamed her workers."

"If she stole it, what's her motivation?" I asked. "She's already rich."

"She wants money without her husband knowing about it."

That seemed reasonable. "How can we prove it? And in time to get paid for the rent money?"

Zinnia waved her hand. "We gonna have to beg, borrow, and . . ." She had started to say "steal," and we both began giggling. Everything seemed funny that morning.

In my mind I still remembered seeing Big Mama naked.

"What about Dr. Williams?" I said. "Suppose he stole his own money so he wouldn't have to pay the plumber?"

"Two thousand dollars for a plumber?" asked Zinnia. "You could build a whole house full of plumbing for that! Now, I could check that out. I pass his medical office and drink his 'colored water' coming home from work."

"But that ain't the way home," I said.

"I come that way."

"Why?"

"To see what's at the white movie shows."

"Oh." I had known that she liked to look at the movie stars' pictures outside the movies for whites only. Sometimes our three movie theaters for colored people didn't carry the same pictures.

"You?" I was accusing her of stealing. Our style of talk. She looked startled, then asked, "Motivation?"

"New dresses." We both broke up giggling.

"You!" she said.

"Motivation?" I asked.

"Rent money."

We stopped laughing. She knew how I worried about the rent.

"I'll ask Mr. Greendale if I can work extra." I didn't have much hope. I already did everything that needed to be done.

We heard Big Mama sit up and drag her slippers on the floor. We smelled the minty liniment she rubbed on her back.

Zinnia said, pointing at me, "You check out Big Mama, and talk to Mrs. Louise Cook."

She pointed to herself. "I'll talk to the cleaning man at Dr. Williams's medical office."

I nodded. Now, how was I going to get all the way across town and back before or after working for Mr. Greendale? By bus, it would have been easy. But we were talking walking.

Before the boycott we wouldn't have dared to try to find the true thief. Now I couldn't "passively accept" the accusation. Besides, the sooner someone found that money, the sooner we could get paid. We had been expecting two or three dollars apiece, then we'd almost have the ten dollars we needed.

A neighborhood dog, scratching fleas, thumped under the house. Busy mockingbirds sang greetings. And I felt ready to investigate, walking or not.

After breakfast of corn bread and water, I caught Zinnia by the elbow. "We have another problem, you know."

She raised her eyebrows. "What?"

"The problem of who steals the money out of this house."

She made a face. "You wanna bet?"

"What?" I heard Mama Merryfield close the door.

"I bet Big Mama knows all about it," said Zinnia.

"Just like you think she knows all about our mother?" I shouldn't have said that. Zinnia really needed to know our mother.

"I dream about her every night," Zinnia said with a

smile. "She wears dangling earrings and high-heel red shoes."

"High-heel shoes?" I said. "Then she sure ain't sticking with the bus boycott."

"She drives a long, shiny car, fool."

I straightened up and clenched my teeth. "If she's so rich, and owns a car, how come she lets her children stay with her poor, old grandmother? And they can't even pay the rent!"

A phantom mother who never checked up on her children and never helped out with rent money was no mother to me. Susan Merryfield was just a name, not a person I could care about.

On the other hand, Mama Merryfield kept us in Christian Sunday school and at prayer meetings. She taught us manners. She made us attend church, and the MIA meetings. Because of Mama Merryfield, anytime the churches needed help, we were called.

Way back in December me and Zinnia had helped pass out the handbills that let people know about this bus boycott.

No, I didn't need Susan Merryfield. I turned my back on Zinnia and we walked our separate ways to work.

After work, I ached all over. I was definitely dragging as I left Mr. Greendale, yet I had to go to the yellow house. I had promised Zinnia. Those buses passing me were tempting, and I had dimes in my pocket. My knee hurt extra from kneeling on windowsills washing windows. So I was limping when a deacon from our church passed in a car. I waved and called.

He slowed down. I ran and tapped his door. "Please, sir," I asked, "I need a ride."

After I crawled in beside him, I said, "Sir, I'm going over to Dr. Williams's house. I want to see Mrs. Louise Cook. Could you take me anywhere near there?" Of course I was already in his long, black car that smelled of leather and silver polish.

"Sure. Always have a ride for Mama Merryfield's children. I pick up lots of folks in town," he said. "We offered Mama Merryfield rides from work, but she say she be walking for her dignity."

"Yes, sir." Walking for her dignity and getting lost!

"See this here map?" he asked.

"Yes, sir."

"We mostly pick up old folks, mens and womens, and the crippled, and ladies who gonna have babies. That there's my route tonight. The colored postal workers mapped the city for us, pickup points and all."

"Yes, sir."

"Know where I got the car?" He was grinning with teeth that were yellow and mostly absent, but his grin was kind. I had wondered about the car. I knew he didn't own it; and he drove a truck for his white boss.

"No, sir."

"The day after we started the taxi runs for helping colored folks to work and back, my boss called me in. He say, 'George, you know how to drive?' I say, 'Yes, sir.' Been driving for him for fifteen years.

"He say, 'Take my car for a taxi. I want you to come in late and leave early. You know what I mean, George?' And I stared at that man. Well, tears come to my eyes. And I say, 'Yes, sir.'

"And he say, 'This is between you and me, George. It's about time things change in Alabama.' And that's how come I got this car."

"Yes, sir." I had heard things like that. Many white people had the courage to help us with the boycott. That was hard for them to do in Montgomery, Alabama, "the Cradle of the Confederacy." This was the town where Jefferson Davis was inaugurated president of the Confederate States of America. The telegram to fire on Fort Sumter and start the War Between the States came from Montgomery. And every time I walked past my favorite fountain in Court Square, I remembered that slaves were sold at auction there.

As our church deacon let me out, I said, "Sir, if you see Mama Merryfield sitting under a tree, make her take a ride home. She's been getting confused and sometimes she gets lost."

"I be doing that, son. And God bless you."

"Thank you, sir."

Walking, I never would have made it to the yellow house before Mrs. Cook left for the day. Even with the ride, I reached the driveway just as she walked out.

I waved to her. She signaled for me to walk on and she would catch up with me. When Dr. Williams's car passed, I understood: She didn't want us to be seen together. She caught up.

"Alfa," she said, "there be something mighty strange going on at that yellow house."

"Yes, ma'am."

"How's your Mama Merryfield?"

"Pretty good, ma'am."

"Did you see Mrs. Williams's face yesterday?"

"No, ma'am. Well, yes, ma'am."

"She be feeling bad about that money. Her no-good brother been hanging around the house when Dr. Williams ain't there. I be betting he sneaked into the kitchen and stole that money."

"Yes, ma'am."

"And Mrs. Williams know that to be the truth! Well, this be my corner, Alfa. Nice talking to you."

"Yes, ma'am." I stood looking after her. We only had six days until the rent was due. I needed to know more, so I ran.

"Mrs. Cook," I called, "who is Mrs. Williams's brother? What does he look like?"

"Oh"—she glanced around—"y'all know him. He work—when he work—at that corner gas station." She pointed.

Mrs. Williams had a brother who worked at a gas station? "His name, ma'am?" I needed facts.

"Why, he be an Adams like she were. Paul Adams."

"Yes, ma'am. Thank you, ma'am." I started back.

"Alfa," she called, raising her hand.

Turning, I said, "Ma'am?"

"Don't do no asking questions. Swear to God, I didn't see nobody that morning. And Paul Adams be part of them neo-Nazi people. Be careful of them. And don't say nothing 'bout me."

"Yes, ma'am. No, ma'am. Thank you, ma'am." Now I had something to tell Zinnia, so I could go home; but I was thinking.

I could at least walk by and look at neo-Nazi Paul Adams, who might have stolen the money. Maybe I could hear him talking. Maybe he would be boasting about it. I turned back.

When Mrs. Louise Cook had walked far enough away, I limped toward that gas station.

As I crossed the street, I saw a colored man drive by with five people besides himself stuffed in a car like dressing stuffed in a turkey. I smiled and yet I worried.

I had heard that white police were arresting colored drivers right and left for going too slow, going too fast, stopping their cars, starting their cars. The fines were costly, yet the drivers kept rolling. It made gooseflesh on my arms.

When I reached that gas station, the courage of that driver helped me. I walked up to the attendant and asked, "Is Mr. Paul Adams here, sir? I gots a message for him, sir." I talked differently for this white man.

"Well, Nigra, y'all out of luck. Paul Adams got him some sudden cash, and split town. We won't see him back 'till he run outta money." He laughed.

I nodded. "Thank you, sir." My back felt his eyes burning on it like a branding iron as I walked away.

"Say, Nigra," he called, "what message?"

Without answering, I limped away, bending under a

mimosa tree that lifted a thousand puffs of pink. Really sweating now, I walked on, being careful not to step on cracks in the sidewalk.

That night after eating a bread-and-butter sandwich, I lay down. Zinnia was out with her friends. Big Mama fell to sleep early. The next morning, I thought, I would have plenty to tell Zinnia. As I fell asleep, I wondered what she had learned.

CHAPTER NINE

Five days until the rent money was due, and I hadn't figured out how to make up the ten dollars. This time, I woke Zinnia.

She was dressed in a jiffy. "Well, I learned a lot," she said. We sat shoulder to shoulder in the back doorway, whispering. The mosquitoes weren't bad that morning because there was a steady breeze. It seemed to be blowing up some summer rain.

"What?" I asked.

"There hasn't been any plumbing job at Dr. Williams's medical office, but everything's leaking. The cleaning woman said two ceiling tiles are broken, and the office hasn't been painted in five years."

"Why?"

"She says Dr. Williams is stingy with his money. He hasn't paid his help in two months."

"But," I said, "he tosses two thousand dollars in a silver clip on his kitchen shelf and leaves it all morning? That doesn't sound like someone who's stingy."

"Maybe he forgot it."

"How could anyone forget two thousand dollars? Even for a white doctor, that must be hard. Stingy people don't throw money around."

"Remember, he said he needed it for the plumber," Zinnia said. "Now, if there ain't a plumber, he was lying. That makes him a stronger suspect."

"Suspect? Why would Dr. Williams steal his own money? Besides, if things are leaking, he does need a plumber." I frowned. "But people don't generally pay before the plumber does the work."

"Maybe he left the money for folks to see, came back for it, and let people think it was stolen," she said.

"Why?" I asked. "And remember, he didn't call the police. Mrs. Williams did."

"Alfa, when you work on solving a problem, everything is suspect. The least likely person is usually the thief."

"Everything and everybody?"

"Right."

"Well," I said, "listen to this. I happen to know that Dr. Williams has a brother-in-law named Paul Adams, Mrs. Williams's brother. He works at a gas station, and hangs around the yellow house when Dr. Williams ain't there."

"So?"

"He's poor. Hangs out with the neo-Nazis. And besides that, I went to the gas station where he works." Pausing, I let that sink in. Zinnia seemed impressed.

"You went to the gas station where a neo-Nazi works?"

"And when I asked for him, the attendant laughed and said he wouldn't be around for a while because he had some money."

"Money? So you think he stole it?"

I shrugged. "I don't have proof. And he's gone, so what good does that do us?" The breeze grew cooler and damp. It smelled of magnolia blossoms and felt good on my face.

"Yeah," Zinnia said. "We're right back where we started."

"And five days until July first."

Big Mama was up. Zinnia took my hand, and we stood around the corner of the house. Big Mama passed to go to the outhouse and never noticed us.

"Say," I said, "we suspected Big Mama."

"Let's search while she's out," said Zinnia. "She acts so strange. I never know what she might do."

"But she'll be back in a minute."

We heard her drop the latch. When she'd be there for a while, she locked the door. We tiptoed into the house.

I reached for my flashlight and pushed the switch. As we knelt by Big Mama's bed, I ran the light everywhere. Zinnia checked the sheets and pillowcase. She pointed under the bed.

"You said you saw something in her shoes."

I was almost afraid to look. Five shoes shook out dirt and pebbles. The sixth shoe rustled, then paper fell out. Green paper folded small. My heart stopped.

Zinnia held the paper in the light. Her hands trembled. I was relieved to see that the paper had been folded several times.

"A handbill," said Zinnia, "for a pawnshop."

That didn't make sense. I turned it over. On the back was a map and directions showing how to reach the places Big Mama worked on different days, and how to get back home.

Her handwriting was beautiful. Big Mama had finished Tuskegee Institute in her youth. Some of her directions on the map were in "shorthand." She had had commercial training, typing and stenography. But because of the System, she couldn't get the kind of job she was prepared for. Nobody hired colored folks in offices in Montgomery, except to clean them. If we got to college, we might have to leave Alabama to make a decent living.

Zinnia moaned and shook her head. "Poor Mama Merryfield," she said. "She's trying not to get lost. This is her map."

"That's sad," I said, nodding. "A map to show her around a city she knows by heart."

"Not really. Remember, we used to ride the buses? She could travel on the Montgomery buses. Walking, I even find myself turned around."

"Or facing tough white boys."

"They still bothering you?"

"They yell things. I call their names and say, 'Hello.'"

"You talk to them?" Zinnia looked at me as if I had said I talked to monsters from the moon.

"They're people."

"They're animals."

I knew how she felt. Sometimes as I passed them I hated their guts. But if you were nonviolent, you saw everyone as a child of God. And I sure wanted those white boys to see me that way. 'Walk the walk and talk the talk in the manner of love.'

"You've attended too many MIA meetings," my sister said. She understood about nonviolence; she just didn't believe it. While talking, we had forgotten about Big Mama. She walked in as we knelt by her bed. I flashed my light on our faces so she'd know who we were.

"What you children praying for?" She grunted as she lowered herself on the bed. We had sold her four-poster wedding bed for two months' rent when we'd been sick with flu and couldn't work. Now Big Mama slept on a narrow cot, the same as we did.

I held out the half-folded map. "Where'd you get the pawnshop handbill?"

She looked frightened. "Is somebody looking for it? Big Mama just used it for a little writing."

"That's all right," I told her. "I just wondered."

She stared at the green handbill. "I reckon it was at the yellow house. I had some time, and my mind was clear. So I did a little writing."

I raised my eyebrows. So Mama Merryfield knew

that sometimes her mind wasn't clear. How hard that must be.

Mama Merryfield's face crumpled up, and she shook her head. "I sure hope that new Reverend King is right," she said, "and we can change the System. So hard-hearted white people don't all go to hell."

"I never heard you talk like that," I said. I was shocked.

"I'm getting old. And since the boycott, I been thinking. The ladies at every house where I clean scold me because I walk. Tell me I got there late. Mrs. McDermott said I was late, and it was because I wasn't taking the bus. She carried on about Communists in Montgomery stirring up trouble among the colored people. And how happy we colored people had been before Mrs. Rosa Parks was 'put up to' staying in her seat."

Mrs. McDermott was almost as old as Mama Merryfield. White people drew "social security" when they grew old. Could old colored people do the same? I should find out.

Big Mama took a breath before going on. "I was so worried. After I put on my uniform, I looked at her kitchen clock. I looked at her dining room clock. Both clocks said it was only ten of eight o'clock. I was ten minutes early, not late! Then to put the last nail in my coffin, she said I couldn't use a mop on her floors anymore. She made me get down on my old knees and scrub her dog-gone kitchen.

"So," said Big Mama, "I drew myself a map so I can

be even faster walking." She moaned. "Walking up and down these hills, an old lady can get turned around."

I hugged her. "Mama Merryfield," I said, "it's all right to get turned around walking. I find myself swearing I never saw the stores in front of me before. It's hard now that we ain't riding the buses."

I kissed her on the cheek. Her wrinkled brown skin was soft and smelled of lavender soap.

"Well," said Zinnia, "be sure to use your map."

"But," I added quickly, "if you get lost, we'll find you." Before I folded that map, I checked the address. The pawnshop wasn't far from Greendale Grocery.

I decided to look in the pawnshop window that morning. Maybe there would be something around our house I could pawn for rent money. July 1 was near.

CHAPTER TEN

That morning as I stacked melons outside Greendale Grocery with the Alabama sun scalding my back, I wondered about Paul Adams. I had been at every window in the yellow house. I had changed wash water and rinse water several times in the kitchen. And in all that time, I never saw a stranger who could have been Mrs. Williams's brother, Paul Adams.

In fact, I could tell when that money clip must have disappeared; I'd say it was about eleven o'clock. Mrs. Louise Cook had been preparing meals then. She would have seen him for sure. She even knew who he was.

Did she take the money? Why did she tell me about Mrs. Williams's brother? Was she trying to keep me from suspecting her? Or was she covering up for Paul

Adams? Why didn't she want me to ask questions? On the other hand, the station attendant did say Paul Adams had "sudden cash."

After I sprayed the spinach and collard greens with the hose, I raced around, restacking shelves. Instead of lifting, I pushed my box of cans because my knee really hurt. I was finished for lunch by eleven-thirty.

"Mr. Greendale," I said, "could I take my lunch break early?"

"Y'all making a lot of demands now that y'all boycotting our good Montgomery buses."

"Yes, sir."

"Y'all gonna start taking the buses soon? I'm tired of you coming in late."

"Sorry, sir." I had never been late, and he knew it.

He pointed as a bus passed with three white ladies and a white man riding. "Empty," he said.

"Yes, sir. Almost."

"I said, empty!"

"Really, sir?" He frowned. Should I have agreed?

Sometimes I daydreamed that Mr. Greendale was old and ill. And he would see me in a white doctor-jacket with a stethoscope around my neck. He would beg pardon for the way he had treated me, and I'd forgive him.

Dr. King said, "Truth pressed down to earth, will rise again." Mr. Greendale and I both knew the truth. To that date, I had never been late. I shook my head and frowned.

He grinned at me. "What's wrong with y'all, Alfred?"

I hadn't talked back, but I had frowned. I glanced

around the store. No one was there. "I'm learning to 'put up my dukes,' sir."

He laughed and waved me out of the store.

Although Mr. Greendale often upset me, as a boss he was better than most. He always paid on payday, and he kept us in food. In back I had a box full of food for that evening. And he wanted me to add milk and some pork chops before I left. The cornflakes from the box he had slit would taste wonderful with milk. I figured I was lucky to work for Mr. Greendale.

But if I was going to see about raising money for the rent, I had to use that lunch break. And soon I'd have to check up on social security. Usually at lunch I sat in the stuffy storage room and read a biology book. I was memorizing the bones and muscles of the human body. Every doctor needs to know them.

Now I was free. With a hand I brushed my hair for sawdust packing or paper strips, and I headed for that pawnshop.

Blue Boy alighted in my hair. I lifted him off, hoping that he hadn't pooped. Animals are dear to me; they never hurt my feelings or segregate me. But sometimes they make problems. I held the pigeon's hot body to my cheek for a second before he flew off.

While buses passed empty, I hobbled painfully downhill to the pawnshop. What did we have that I could pawn? When I looked in the pawnshop window and saw picture frames, I knew.

On our wall was Mama Merryfield's photograph of her husband. It was in a handsome oval frame. I could pawn the frame for rent money, and buy it back as soon as I could. How much could I get for it? I wondered. It was an antique, some kind of carved wood with gold paint brushed over it. True, it was the only decent thing in our house, but keeping the house was more important.

I stared at other picture frames in that window. There were also pieces of jewelry, fireplace fixings, even a pearl-handled pistol. At the base of the pistol I saw something that stopped my heart.

A silver money clip. Dr. Williams's silver money clip! It was definitely his because it had the initials SLW on it, and there were those snakes. That was my test. What was the possibility of finding two money clips like that in Montgomery?

What was it doing in a pawnshop? Did whoever had stolen the money decide to get money for the clip, too? Of course. A silver clip with someone else's initials couldn't be used by a thief.

The pawnshop handbill had been at the Williams' yellow house. Big Mama had used it to draw her map. Why did a rich household need a pawnshop handbill? Who had brought the handbill there—Mrs. Williams? Mrs. Louise Cook? Paul Adams? Dr. Williams?

But the doctor or his wife wouldn't pawn the clip, would they? That seemed to remove them from the list of suspects.

If only Zinnia were with me, I thought. She would know what to do. I supposed a real scientist would take a snapshot of the clip. As if I owned a camera!

However, I could imagine myself slipping a big black

camera from a tan camera bag on my back. I'd whistle, and a dozen sleek, black dogs would mill and yelp around me. While people stared at the big dogs, I would stoop and click off photos. I'd turn the camera this way and that, snapping pictures. Then, at a signal, I'd walk off, and the dogs would slip away in all directions. I saw that in a movie once.

Back to reality. I could ask the salesman inside if he knew who brought the clip in. Even if he only knew whether it was a man or a woman, that would help.

A woman could be Mrs. Louise Cook, or Mrs. Williams. I wouldn't even consider Zinnia or Mama Merryfield, even though I got the pawnshop handbill from Mama Merryfield. A man could be Mrs. Williams's brother, Paul Adams, or Dr. Williams.

Of course, it was ridiculous to consider Dr. Williams. He was a doctor living in a mansion on a hillside. Being stingy—as his help said—just meant that he took care of his money.

A bus passed, and I glanced up. A colored lady sat with a white child on her lap. She couldn't help taking the bus. I smiled to make her feel better. She pointed to the child's yellow curls, and I nodded.

I waited until there was no one in the pawnshop. Never in my life had I been in a pawnshop. The silver clip almost made me forget pawning our oval picture frame. Maybe I could ask about both?

Just as I was ready to go in, a lady went in. I think she got back a gold watch because I saw it on the counter. When she left, I walked in. The shop smelled like apples with cinnamon. The man behind the counter looked at me, and behind me.

"Whatcha want, Nigra? You look like one of the Commies making trouble round here."

"Sir," I asked, "I want to know how much money you would give me for an old picture frame."

"Did you steal it?" He snickered and leaned on his elbows.

"No, sir, it has my great-grandfather's picture in it."

"Why y'all wanna pawn it, then?"

"We need money to pay the rent, sir."

"So, how can I tell you how much money without seeing it?"

"Yes, sir. I'll bring it in, sir."

"You talking mighty fancy. You still in school, boy?"

"Yes, sir."

"Ain't gonna do you no good, you know."

"Yes, sir."

"Nothing worse than an uppity, educated nigger."

"Yes, sir." I turned. "Sir, I was wondering about that money clip in the window." I pointed.

"You think it belong to y'all?"

"No, sir, but I think I know who it does belong to."

"Then it ain't none of your business, now is it?"

"Sir, could you tell me if a man or a woman brought it in to pawn, sir?" My legs wanted to run out, but my head stayed in that shop. I needed to clear our names.

He frowned. "I said, it ain't none of your business. I'll tell the person whose business it is."

"Thank you, sir." Turning, I walked out. A breeze

outside made me feel better. It was beginning to sprinkle.

I glanced at an antique clock in the pawnshop window. If it was right, I had fifteen minutes to get to Dr. Williams's office, tell him where his money clip was, and get back to Greendale Grocery.

If only I had Blue Boy's wings!

CHAPTER ELEVEN

Outside the pawnshop, I stared around. Which way had I come? Mama Merryfield wasn't the only one who could get lost. I limped to the corner to read the street signs. I had gone the wrong way. Embarrassed, I turned and ran.

Suddenly, I stopped, seeing a rusty black bicycle with one low tire. It looked as if someone had thrown it away, there beside the street. If I took it, I could bring it back. Or leave it. Would the police say I stole it? I had to hurry so, jumping on, I rode that bike in the drizzle like an eagle flying.

People stared at me as I rode thumping along. I could be stopped as a thief even if what I was riding had been thrown away. I had to ride fast.

When I passed a shop that had a water fountain for

colored, I straddled the bike to drink. I hadn't eaten since morning, and I felt dizzy. The refreshing drink made me feel better.

I had always been grateful to the shops that provided a water fountain for colored people. After all, it cost twice the money to put in two fountains.

Lately I had realized that my colored mouth wasn't a threat to anyone. Reverend King said the System of separate things for colored and white was a way of making us colored feel bad about ourselves.

Suddenly I laughed.

Suppose the water really was a different color? Suppose a rainbow of sweet water came from the "colored" fountain, and it was the fountain of youth? But only colored people were allowed to drink it. And white people were angry with their old, clear water. Wouldn't that be something!

I reached Dr. Williams's office driveway just as he got out of his car. I rested the bike against a wall. I had ten minutes to tell him where his money clip was, and to get back to Greendale Grocery, which was at least twenty minutes away.

I straightened my black bow tie. Glancing down, I realized my white shirt clung to my undershirt and skin, and my brown pants were soaked from riding in the drizzle.

"Dr. Williams, sir," I said, keeping a respectful distance from him, "I'm trying to clear our names from being accused of stealing your two thousand dollars. And we need that pay for rent money." I took a deep breath.

He glanced around and loosened his necktie. "Hush. Lower your voice."

I looked around, too. His nurse was standing in the doorway waiting for him with a folder. No one else could hear me.

"Yes, sir," I said. Then in a lower voice, "Sir, I was just at the pawnshop downtown, and I saw your silver money clip. I know it's yours, sir, because it has 'SLW' on it."

Dr. Williams just stared at me. He stared at me like a man who had never seen a colored boy before. Then his upper lip curled, and he frowned as if I were an Alabama cockroach. "You got yourself a mighty big nose, now ain't you, Alfa?"

"Sir?"

"Whose business is it where my silver clip is?"

Before the boycott I would have apologized and backed away. Now I stood tall. "Sir," I said slowly, "it's my business when your wife accuses us of stealing it."

"How do I know that you didn't pawn my clip?"

Oh, I thought, this is ridiculous. "Dr. Williams, the pawnshop owner will tell you who pawned your clip. Maybe he knows about your money, too."

I walked away without being dismissed, which was bold. Over my shoulder I called, "And we need our pay, sir."

By accident I walked in the wrong direction, but I wasn't about to let him know that. I hadn't heard him slam the car door, so I limped straight ahead with head high, and turned the corner.

There, I peeked around the building. When I saw him go in, I hobbled back down the street to the bicycle and his office. The rain had stopped, and oil slicks made rainbows on the street. As I passed the office door, I heard a *hiss*.

"Come here, boy," his nurse said. She stepped out of the antiseptic-smelling office.

"Ma'am?"

"Tell me. What's this about a pawnshop?" Her eyes were very blue, her face very white, and her lipstick was a bright red. I wondered if patients thought they saw blood on her lips?

Maybe they would think that she was a vampire and sucked blood. Were her teeth pointed? If I were a patient at that office, I'd watch when that nurse drew my blood for tests. I'd make sure she didn't drink any.

She had asked about the pawnshop. Should I mind my own business, or should I tell her? She probably knew Dr. Williams well. If only Zinnia were there.

"Ma'am," I began.

"What? Tell me. I want to know." She closed the office door and crossed her arms.

"Does Dr. Williams have trouble with money, ma'am? Because my great-grandmother ain't been paid for working for him. And we were blamed when he lost some money."

"Money?" She rolled her blue eyes. "This evening I'm handing in my resignation. Let me tell you. I ain't been paid-in-full for months. It's a little here, and a little there."

"Why would he have two thousand dollars in cash, ma'am?"

"To pay his gambling debts. That's what they tell me. That man's addicted to gambling. But, tell me, what's this about a pawnshop?"

"The silver money clip he had had two thousand dollars in, ma'am. I just saw it at the pawnshop."

"I thought so. The doctor must have pawned it himself. He's that hard up for money." She shook her head, then smiled. "Ain't you one of Aunt Lydia Merryfield's children?"

"Yes, ma'am."

"Well, give my regards to Aunt Lydia. Tell her Mrs. Mary Brown says hello. Good-bye, Merryfield."

"Good-bye, ma'am."

Dr. Williams gambled? He didn't pay his office people? Not even the white ones? Maybe his wife planned the whole police thing to get us to clean her house for free?

I returned uphill to Greendale Grocery as fast as that old bike would take me. As I passed the pawnshop window, I glanced in. The silver money clip was gone. My heart did a flip-flop.

I left the bike on the street not too far from where I found it, and hobbled the rest of the way.

CHAPTER TWELVE

On my way back to Greendale Grocery, I passed blocks of crepe myrtle trees blooming red. I liked to touch their smooth, silvery trunks. The sun would peep out for a few seconds, then hide behind lavender clouds again.

At the grocery, I slipped in the storage room and put on the apron. Mr. Greendale chose not to scold me, or didn't know I was late returning from lunch. I wasn't sure which.

That night I took Zinnia in the yard to talk. We talked behind the outhouse because we had to hide from Big Mama. The stink was awful, but if you stay still, your nose stops smelling any odor, good or bad. I knew that from my biology books.

Five of my dog pals bumped against my legs for joy.

Each dog wanted a pat and a scratch behind its flea-bitten ears.

I was really proud of black-and-white Tramp, who walked on three legs. I had been there when a truck broke his hind leg. He would have bled to death if I hadn't saved him. Luckily the dog was unconscious. I took a handsaw to that femur bone, then sewed the skin. I soaked that stump day after day to make sure there was no infection.

The neighbors on the block had been astonished. "That boy really should be a doctor," they had said.

Now I shooed the dogs away, and Zinnia and I sat on crates. "Zinnia," I said, "today I found more evidence than I ever wanted to have."

"Like what?"

"Well, remember that pawnshop advertised on the handbill?"

She nodded.

"I visited there. The good news is that we could pawn Great-grandfather Merryfield's picture frame and we would get enough to pay the rent. I think."

She shook her head. "Those pawn-shop people are criminals. They never give you as much money as things are worth, and then they turn around and sell your property for a big price. When you go to get it back, it's gone. Some of my friends have pawned things."

She had soured my cream. What could I say after that?

"Go on," she said, "I'm sorry. We'll do whatever we have to for rent money."

"I know." I shook my head. "That picture's Big Mama's treasure. The only thing of value left here."

Zinnia said, "An old lady told me that when they used to have dance competitions, Lydia and Marcus always won, dancing the Charleston. Big Mama danced in a short red dress with black fringe. The lady said you should have seen them kick up their heels."

"Knowing Big Mama, I can imagine that."

We were both quiet for a time. I was thinking that we were lucky to have a great-grandmother like Lydia Merryfield. She was crazy, but she really loved us.

That's why it was such a shame that she had been accused of stealing. The System being what it was, I was sure it wasn't the first time she had been falsely accused. However, it was the first time Alfa Merryfield was involved.

"Zinnia," I said, "I'm gonna clear her name if it kills me."

"Don't say that 'if it kills me.'" She looked frightened. "What's the bad news if that was the good news?"

"Yeah," I said, "the bad news is that I saw Dr. Williams's silver money clip in the pawnshop window."

"You didn't!"

"I did."

"Well, that's good news." She stared at me. "What does it mean?"

"I tried to find out who brought it in."

"They wouldn't tell you?"

"Man said he'd tell the person whose business it was."

"Whoa!" Zinnia said. "Did he say it that way?"

I nodded.

"That means that the pawnshop person knew it wasn't the property of the person pawning it."

My mouth flew open. "You're right! The doctor's nurse thinks he pawned it. Way to go, Zinnia. The man said it wasn't my business, but the business of the person who owned it."

"He knew."

"So, where does that leave us?" Zinnia was good at this. She snapped her fingers. "We have to go tell Dr. Williams."

"I told him already."

She looked impressed. "And?"

"He basically told me to mind my own business."

"Oh, oh, he knows more than he's saying. Listen to what I heard." She crossed her arms. "At work I heard some white people joking. This man said in the old world they had to 'pay the piper,' but now in Montgomery they had to 'pay the plumber.'"

I stared at her. Whatever she meant passed over my head.

"Pay the plumber, don't you see?"

I wrinkled my nose.

"Remember, Dr. Williams said he had to 'pay the plumber?'"

"And you think that means something besides paying the man who fixes sinks, drainpipes, and water faucets?"

"Maybe it does."

"Well, yeah, but I didn't tell you my whole story. After telling Dr. Williams about the money clip, it disappeared from the pawnshop window!"

"The shop manager probably took it out. Maybe he was waiting for Dr. Williams to come for it."

"I never said his name."

"He'd know it belonged to a doctor with the initials SLW."

"How?"

"The caduceus. That winged stick with two snakes wound around it. That's the symbol of the medical profession, and what other doctor in Montgomery is SLW?"

I remembered seeing that thing with the two snakes. My sister knew a lot. I was proud of her. "And something else," I said.

"What?"

"Dr. Williams's nurse says he has lots of gambling debts."

"That's interesting. We have to go over our suspects," she said. "But first, let's ask Mama Merryfield who 'the plumber' is."

CHAPTER THIRTEEN

I followed Zinnia inside the house.

Mama Merryfield was reading a psalm aloud. When she finished, she closed her eyes and sat in prayer. Zinnia shook her shoulder. I wouldn't have disturbed her, but Zinnia was businesslike.

"Big Mama," she asked, "if someone said to you 'pay the plumber,' what would you think?"

I watched Big Mama look around and come back to earth. I suppose she had been 'talking to the Lord,' as she called it, and now she had to answer Zinnia's question. "We don't need a plumber," she said. "We ain't got any pipes, child."

"Not us. Anybody."

"Then let them call the plumber, and pay him, too."

I decided to try. "Big Mama, is there somebody in Montgomery who is known as 'the plumber?'"

"Sure is, and you stay away from him, young man." She stared at me. "Are you visiting my little Zinnia?"

"Big Mama, I'm Alfa. Alfa, your great-grandson."

"Where is Alfa? Has he come home this evening?"

"Yes, Big Mama." It really hurt when she didn't recognize me. Her mind seemed to come and go.

"Why should I stay away from the plumber?" I asked.

"Because he collects money, child. He's what they call a 'loan shark.' He lends to them gambling men, then collects with big interest." She shook her head. "That Mr. Plumber is a mean son of Adam. When I walk by his house, I shake the dust from my feet."

Well, there it was. What I remembered about Mr. Fred Plumber were his long, thin legs and slender body, like a tap dancer. He drove a dark gray car that looked like a funeral car, because you couldn't see in the back.

"Go to bed, Mama Merryfield," said Zinnia. My sister was bossy. Not only bossy, but mean sometimes. Big Mama knew what to do and when to do it.

"Thank you, dear," said Big Mama. "I'll just sit and pray until my great-grandchildren come in. They're late this evening. Poor little gems, they work so hard to help their Mama Merryfield."

Before Zinnia could begin scolding her, I covered my sister's mouth with my hand and dragged her from the room. She put up a fight, but I was strong. As I passed my bed, I reached for my precious flashlight.

Could I pawn it for rent money? I would if I needed to.

Next, I dragged Zinnia out the back door and around the house. When we walked in the front door, I slammed it loudly, and elbowed big-mouth Zinnia.

"Hi, Big Mama," she yelled.

I flashed light in both our faces. "We're home," I called.

"Thank the Lord," said Mama Merryfield. "Zinnia and Alfa are home. Now I can go to bed." I hugged Big Mama and kissed her good night.

This time when I covered Zinnia's mouth with my hand, she bit me. It was clear that she didn't believe in nonviolence. However, I didn't want her to say anything more to Big Mama.

Out back again, Zinnia took pencil to paper. "Let's see who our suspects are. Hold that flashlight steady."

"The same as before," I said, "don't you think?"

"Hush, Alfa. It's completely different now. We have two new people."

"Oh, sure, you mean besides Paul Adams, maybe Mr. Plumber came in the yellow house kitchen and stole the money?"

"Suppose the money wasn't there to steal?" Zinnia said. "Suppose Dr. Williams tossed out the money, then had it taken. Now he has an excuse for not paying his gambling debts. What about that, huh?"

"Whoa, back up. Dr. Williams had it stolen?"

"Everybody saw the money in the silver money clip, right? A policeman knows it was there, and that it disappeared. There's even a police report. So, if Mr. Plumber demanded two thousand dollars on that day, Dr. Williams could claim it was stolen. And he might still have the money."

"Who took it and gave it back to him? That's pretty strange, don't you think?"

"Maybe he stole it from himself."

"Did you see him come back to the house?" I asked. "I clearly saw that money until about eleven o'clock."

Waving her hands, Zinnia said, "Why didn't you say so? That changes everything."

"It does?" To save the batteries, I clicked off the flashlight. Besides, she wasn't writing.

"Sure. Mrs. Louise Cook is their loyal maid. Dr. Williams gives her orders to take the money for him. He pays her fifty cents for helping him. And when anyone asks, she's to mention his brother-in-law."

I sat, amazed at my sister, then I sighed. "In that case, we'll never get paid," I said. "I better take Marcus Merryfield's photo out of that picture frame. It's our only hope to pay the rent."

"You worry too much, Alfa," Zinnia said, getting up. She undressed, bathed under the neighbor's outside faucet, and went to bed. I sat thinking, and scratching mosquito bites.

Worry too much? She was forgetting that I was the only man in the house. I began humming my rent-money blues. Big Mama always said to "hope in the

Lord." Well, I was a church-going boy, and a nonviolent worker, so I changed my lyrics:

"Oh, I'm singing the rent-money blues,
The Alabamy rent-money blues.
I got me a feeling, deep down inside,
A big change is walking down the road."

CHAPTER FOURTEEN

The next morning I woke before dawn, knowing we had exactly four days until the rent was due. I was glad that I could pawn that picture frame.

Moonlight was silken in the air that June morning. In the refreshing cool, birds were calling, insects were chirping, and tree frogs were whistling.

We had a screwdriver, pliers, and a kitchen knife. I figured I'd need all three. I had to remove that photo carefully and not scratch the picture frame. I had wanted to ask Zinnia to hold the flashlight for me. But she and Big Mama were still sleeping, and I figured I could work by moonlight.

Our next-door neighbor looked out his window. As I waved at him, he waved and disappeared. We had good

neighbors. Almost everybody down the street was rent-
ing a house from Mr. Harris, but most were fancy four-
room homes with porches, electricity, and indoor
bathrooms.

Our tar-paper house embarrassed the street, but the
neighbors loved Mama Merryfield. Because she lived
there, they didn't mind the house so much. Big Mama
had nursed them in sickness and cheered them in sorrow.

That photo frame was strong wood. At the back, little
nails held musty-smelling, crumbling paper for a first
layer. Under the paper was brown cardboard that looked
fresh. I tried to pull out the nails, but they stuck in the
wood frame. Then I looked carefully at the cardboard
and realized the nails did not have to come out.

Someone had been slipping that cardboard out in a
slit at the side of the frame. I stared at it in wonder. Did
Big Mama perhaps take out her husband's photo from
time to time? But as I searched, I saw that between two
sheets of cardboard there were letters. I pulled them
out. One envelope had a return address to Diamond
Merryfield, our grandfather, in New York City. My
hands trembled.

Another letter was from Susan Merryfield, our
mother, in Atlanta, Georgia. The postmark was from
four years ago. So Zinnia was right; Mama Merryfield
did know more than she had told us.

When I heard people moving in our house, I slipped
the letters and cardboards back into the frame. I decided
not to tell Zinnia, because she was too emotional. After
work that evening I'd read the letters first, and empty the

frame. Then I would show the letters to Zinnia. We still had four days. The pawnshop would be open all week.

That morning I worked at Greendale Grocery in a daze. What did the letters tell Mama Merryfield? Had she written her son, Diamond, asking for help? So our mother was in Georgia. What did she do for a living? My thoughts spun like a musical merry-go-round while I kept my hands busy straightening cans on every shelf in the store.

It was a quiet morning. Only two people came in for food. Some people shopped at the big supermarkets. I lined up lemons and limes, alternating yellow and green.

"Albert," said Mr. Greendale, "seems to me y'all making work where work ain't due."

"Yes, sir."

"Not that I mind."

"Yes, sir."

When I finished, my hands smelled of lemon and lime oils. Mr. Greendale shook his head. "Alfred, go take your lunch break. If y'all straighten another thing in this store, I'll have to leave."

"Yes, sir." After sweeping the floor and spraying the greens, I rinsed my face in the hose water. Even the water was hot that morning.

From the front counter, Mr. Greendale called, "I said, Go."

"Yes, sir."

"And take some extra time like y'all did the other day."

I walked into the storage room. So, he had noticed

when I came back late. I wished I could go home to read those letters, but walking would take forty-five minutes each way. I didn't have that much time. Dimes jingled in my pocket—bus fare. The bus would take seven easy minutes each way, but no, I shook my head. I wasn't riding.

After eating a mushy banana for lunch, I opened my biology book. If only I had a notebook to write in. Then I could copy those Latin names of bones and muscles. I was memorizing the spelling, when I heard Mr. Greendale's voice.

"Albert! There's a nigra woman here to see you."

Mrs. Louise Cook stood in the store. She beckoned me out the front door. Squeezing my shoulder, she asked, "Alfa, did y'all say anything to anybody about me?"

"No, ma'am."

The chauffeur for the Williams family sat across the street in one of their cars. Mrs. Cook had gotten a ride.

"They coming down on me hard about that money," she said.

There went Zinnia's solution to the problem. "Yes, ma'am."

Mrs. Cook began crying. "All these years, and half the time not paying me. And they be thinking I stole from Dr. Williams."

"Yes, ma'am." I felt sorry for her. Should I tell her what I knew about the silver money clip, or Dr. Williams's gambling? Who was I to tell a grown lady?

"I'm sorry, ma'am. Is Mrs. Williams angry with you?"

"It be Dr. Williams. And he usually be the reasonable

one, you know? Alfa, I tell you something fishy is going on in that yellow house."

"Yes, ma'am." That really changed the story. Dr. Williams was looking for his money. Maybe that meant he hadn't planned a scheme to lose and then find it, and Zinnia had been wrong. On the other hand, maybe it meant he was letting people know it was lost.

Mrs. Cook lowered her voice. "Today Mrs. Williams be on the phone over an hour. She been trying to find her no-good brother, Paul, you know. She stood up for y'all Merryfields, though."

"Ma'am?"

"She told Dr. Williams not to go bothering Aunt Lydia Merryfield or she might do something else crazy."

"Yes, ma'am." Sounded as if Mrs. Williams didn't think we had stolen the money after all. Poor Mrs. Cook. Had she stolen it? But if she had, would she be at the store talking to me?

With a wave, she got in the front seat of the chauffeured car and drove away. I returned to my biology book in the storage room. Outside had been cooler, but a colored boy couldn't read a book outside without making white people angry. Where were we now with this money problem?

I decided that pawning the photo frame was the only way to get the rent money for July. We wouldn't get any money from Mrs. Williams, and if she wasn't blaming us, why should I try to clear our names?

Why challenge the lions when you're out of the arena?

Closing my eyes, biology book in hand, I repeated the leg bones: femur, tibia, fibula, patella.

"Alfa," called Mr. Greendale.

Was my lunch break finished? Seemed as if I had just sat down. When I reached the door leading into the grocery store, I saw a police car parked in bright sunlight across the street. Inside the shade of the store stood Officer Jimmy Newton.

The policeman pointed to me.

Oh, no! He'd caught me. I had almost forgotten stealing that bicycle. I said, "Yes, sir, I didn't mean to."

He frowned. "Didn't mean to what?"

Who had turned me in? I left it, didn't I? I felt so guilty. "Only a short time, sir."

"Doing what a short time? Do you know why I'm here?" The policeman frowned and glanced at his watch.

Didn't he know? "What you wanted me for, sir."

"Just a short while, what?"

"Yes, sir, and I returned it." I hadn't exactly returned it to where I took it. I stuttered, "Not far."

Officer Newton waved at me. "I don't know what y'all talking about. And I don't have time to find out. Alfa Merryfield, why were you delivering a message to Mrs. Williams's brother, Paul Adams?"

CHAPTER FIFTEEN

"**Sir?**" I answered Officer Newton.

"Right now, Alfa, I have another burglary to investigate." He glanced at his watch again. "But I want to question y'all. Tomorrow morning, be at the police station. Eight o'clock sharp. Y'all hear?"

"Yes, sir." I closed my eyes and leaned against the door frame. When the policeman left, I returned to straightening the store. I could feel Mr. Greendale's eyes on the back of my head. I glanced up.

After a while, he said, "I suppose y'all don't want to talk about it?"

"No, sir." It was too confusing to explain to someone white. I had hoped he wouldn't have found out about it at all.

"If y'all ain't about to talk, I can find out myself."

"Yes, sir."

"Two people came seeing you today. Dr. Williams's maid and Officer Newton. That and y'all been late returning from lunch."

"Yes, sir." Late once. Tears stung my eyes. Three years of honesty, and he was ready to think the worst of me? He didn't even know what we had been accused of. All afternoon I wiped down walls.

Why had I told that lie? I had let the gas station attendant think I had a message for Mr. Paul Adams, when I didn't. I didn't even know Mr. Paul Adams. Now I was going to suffer because of my little white lie.

Suppose Paul Adams did steal Dr. Williams's two thousand dollars that morning? Maybe Mrs. Cook saw him after all. The fact that I went looking for him seemed to involve me. Maybe the police thought I had stolen the money and given it to him?

Now I had to collect more evidence to prove who took Dr. Williams's money, make a test for who stole from Big Mama, and a third problem was probably home waiting in the photo frame.

All the way home that evening, I trembled. My sore knee ached from my hip to my ankle. I spoke politely to the three white boys who always hung out on the street. They called me names, but they weren't my problem of the moment.

Older people walking home spoke to me and patted my back. "How y'all, Alfa? We proud of you, boy. Stay in school now and make your Mama Merryfield as pleased as a queen bee."

"Yes, sir. Yes, ma'am." What would they think of me when I was arrested for stealing Dr. Williams's money?

My throat was tight. I felt close to tears. I hated to disappoint people. Surely the truth would save me. After all, Mama Merryfield had delivered that policeman at birth, cared for him, and nursed him with her milk. I limped along.

After a while, the colored people walking around me and the green-gold of trees made me feel less worried.

Suppose I talked for a change? Suppose I told everything I knew and suspected to Officer Jimmy Newton? He was a human person. Would anything more horrible happen to me than could happen now?

I tried not to think about Emmett Till.

Before I reached home, I decided not to tell Zinnia about going to the police station the next morning. She would get upset, and Big Mama might find out. Big Mama sensed things when her mind was clear. I didn't want her worrying.

Nobody was home when I arrived. In case I never returned from the police station in the morning, I wrote a note and put it under my pillow. I dated the note for the next day:

> It is three days until the rent is due. This morning I will meet with Officer Jimmy Newton at the police station at 8:00 A.M.

for questioning about **Dr. Williams**'s money.

I love both of you, **Mama Merryfield** and **Zinnia Merryfield**. I did not steal the money.

Alfa Merryfield

Then, all by myself, I took that photo frame to the woods. I wanted to read those letters before showing them to Zinnia. In the woods I found a tree trunk to sit on. This time I slipped the cardboard out easily. Between the two sheets, I saw our mother's letter. I decided to bite the bullet and open it first.

Taking a deep breath, I stared at it. Her handwriting was shaky like an old woman's. She is a human person, I told myself, although I wished I could spit on her. Read the writing "in the manner of love," I told myself.

A letter from only four years before, May 1952, read:

Dear Mama Merryfield,

I'm sorry to hear that you still have money problems. Mr. Plumber should not have given you my address.

Mr. Plumber? Mr. Plumber gave Big Mama our mother's address? What was Big Mama doing, dealing with Mr. Plumber? What was our mother doing, dealing with Mr. Plumber?

Seems you're richer than I am. Last year I made ten thousand and am still in debt. You should be supporting me. Your son, my father, won't help me.

As for those two children, send them to the county. I don't want to see the likes of them unless they can help me with money.

Susan Merryfield

Well, there it was. The answer to Zinnia's dreams. As I stared at the letter, tears began to roll down my cheeks. Inside my heart, I suppose I had always wanted a caring mother who would love me and be proud of me. Now, in a few words, I had learned the truth.

Two later letters at different addresses said about the same thing. One said that we children should be put at a workhouse for juvenile delinquents. But we never got into any trouble before now. How could she say that?

It was growing dark. I knew Big Mama and Zinnia were home, because Zinnia's cooking smelled good, and Mama Merryfield was humming. I had to hurry.

There was a mushy love letter from Marcus to Lydia. He said, "the Lord has brought us together, my precious wife." Some people used the Lord for their own interests, but I suspected Great-grandfather Marcus was sincere.

The one letter from Diamond Merryfield said he was sorry to hear that his sisters Pearl and Ruby had died in a car accident. Car accident? I hadn't known that. What were Merryfields doing in a car?

He said he would try to visit when he could, but that he didn't have money to make it to the funeral. I closed my eyes. No one could help us. All of us Merryfields were poor.

Somehow I had to go to college and break these chains pulling our Merryfield family down. Maybe I could even help support my mother, Susan. But wait, she made ten thousand dollars a year? That was a whole lot of money. Was she a gambler? Where did all that money go?

In my head, I began adding. Our sixty dollars a month combined pay was only seven hundred some dollars a year. Our mother Susy was more wealthy than all three of us. She was like rich white people, moaning about being poor.

Anger bubbled up inside me like red beans at a boil.

White people with money often moaned and groaned about being poor, especially when they went to pay us for working for them. Looking around their homes, I had discovered that they paid for what was important to them.

One lady Big Mama worked for had changed all the furniture in her house three times that I remembered. And another white family paid two hundred dollars for a puppy. The lady said he had "pedigree papers." Pay money for a dog? All the puppies starving in the woods, and all the homeless dogs on the streets, and they paid for a dog?

And Mrs. Williams was a gardener. She had all those fancy foreign plants hanging on the porch of the yellow house, and a forest of trees on the back hillside. Her gardener pulled up good Alabama trees while she paid money for fancy trees from somewhere else.

Funny how rich people spent their money.

I placed the sheets of cardboard back in the photo frame and hid the whole thing in a paper bag. I hoped Big Mama hadn't noticed that it was missing. While she and Zinnia were at the woodstove in the back room, I slipped in the front door and hung the photo on the nail in the wall.

That night we had sausage links and smothered cabbage for dinner. After dinner I went to bed early.

Maybe Officer Newton wasn't like other Alabama policemen. Just because he didn't stop the three white boys from beating me didn't mean that he was unfair. In getting together what I would tell him, I set cans of the story on neat shelves in my mind. All the labels were facing out.

CHAPTER SIXTEEN

As the letter under my pillow said, this morning was now three days before the rent was due. I kept thinking about Emmett Till. As I walked uphill to the police station, I should have been terrified.

However, I was surprised at how different I felt compared to the afternoon at the yellow house when Officer Newton threatened to take us in. Especially since this time I wasn't innocent. I had stolen a bicycle and told a lie.

But, I had a plan. Mr. Greendale had been right: A plan made a big difference. For Officer Newton, I would "put up my dukes," nonviolent dukes, and tell all that I knew.

There were other things I had to think about.

I felt unsure about pawning that photo frame. It was Mama Merryfield's hiding place, and the only thing of real value in our house. Suppose the man at the pawnshop sold it? Dr. Williams's money clip had disappeared. And Zinnia had warned me not to deal with people like that.

Speaking of dealing: Why had Mama Merryfield gone to Mr. Plumber? Only for Susy Merryfield's address? Why did he have our mother's address? Big Mama said she shook the dust from her feet when she passed his house. So, she knew where he lived. But then again, around here most folks knew where other folks lived.

At 7:30 A.M. I slipped into the police station and sat on a hard wooden bench by the door. The bench smelled of sweat and pee, and looked as if it had been there for a hundred years. Police were eating doughnuts and brushing powdered sugar off their uniforms. I remembered that I hadn't eaten or had anything to drink. That was bad. I got dizzy when I didn't eat or drink.

The water fountain said, FOR WHITES ONLY. They needn't have made the sign. Any time a colored person saw one fountain, he knew it was for white people.

My "Walking to the Bus-Rider Blues" ran through my head. I was straightening up when Officer Newton strolled in. Seeing me, he frowned as if he wasn't expecting me.

"Is he your arrest?" a policeman asked. Until then, I hadn't realized anyone had noticed me.

"For interrogation," said Officer Newton. He walked past me. I waited and thought.

At the store Mr. Greendale was stocking shelves all by himself. I hoped he didn't strain his back taking produce off the truck that morning. At least he knew where I was. I waited and waited.

Half an hour later Officer Newton came out and beckoned me to follow him to a room. He sat at one end of a long table—at least ten feet long—and he pointed for me to sit at the other end. I decided not to talk about the stolen bicycle. He probably didn't even know about it.

The wooden table was full of dents and pits, as if people had hammered on it for ages. For a full five minutes by a clock I glanced at, he stared at me.

It amused me to think that I had nothing but my life to lose. I had worked it out in my mind so I didn't have to worry. Without me, Zinnia and Mama Merryfield could move into a house as live-in maids.

Head up, I sat waiting to talk to that policeman.

At last he spoke: "What do y'all have to say for yourself?"

I had been waiting so long, I had everything in order in my mind. As orderly as Mr. Greendale's grocery shelves. I worked my way backward, explaining that my sister Zinnia and I were trying to clear our Merryfield family's names of the accusation. I told him about the following:

The silver money clip showing up in the pawnshop; the importance of the winged snake-stick and SLW initials on the clip; Dr. Williams's attitude and words about his silver clip; Mrs. Louise Cook's suspicion of Paul

Adams; my walk to find him, my little white lie, and the gas station attendant's words about Paul Adams's "sudden cash"; possible meaning of "pay the plumber"; Dr. Williams's office condition; and his nurse's words. I ended this way:

"We Merryfields just have three days. We need money to pay the July rent to Mr. Harris." With that, I wrapped myself in dignity. He could ask me any questions he wanted to.

Then I leaned forward. "And, sir," I said, "I need to find out about social security for colored people."

He stared at me. "The public library is where y'all look things up. I always tell my children to go there."

"Yes, sir." So he had children. I wondered how old they were? Well, he told me to go, so it must be all right.

Officer Newton stared at me for a long time. He pulled out a notebook and wrote in it. Several times he glanced up at me, then he jotted something else in his notebook.

As he wrote, the sky cleared. Not the sky outside— we were in a stuffy inner room—but the sky in my mind. I suddenly knew or suspected who had stolen Dr. Williams's money.

I only needed one additional can to put on the shelf, and I knew where to find that can. This would be Alfa Merryfield's conclusion, done by the scientific method, not Zinnia Merryfield's solving of a mystery, but I think she would approve. Zinnia was fifteen and smart, but I was almost a teenager myself.

Should I, could I, bargain with the policeman?

Boldly, I leaned forward. "Officer Newton, sir, if you help us with ten dollars for our July rent, I'll tell you tomorrow who took Dr. Williams's money. I'm almost sure I know, sir."

He frowned. But Mama Merryfield had pulled him feetfirst from his mama's womb. She had nursed him for half a year. And, I bet she'd never gotten paid. How could you pay someone for that much love? We stared at each other. I held my head high, and my eyes never left his face. I was "talking in the manner of love."

"Ten dollars," he said, pointing at me. "Tomorrow at noon."

I needed to investigate some more. But there was no time today. I needed my job with Mr. Greendale, too. Whatever I did would have to be done tomorrow morning. I could only hope there would be time.

CHAPTER SEVENTEEN

That night when I reached home, I discovered that Mama Merryfield was late. As soon as Zinnia arrived, I opened the photo frame and let her read our mother's letters. If I had told her about them, she never would have believed me.

"Yeah, Alfa," she said sadly.

"You were right," I said, to make her feel better. "Big Mama did know more than she told us."

I put the letters back and hung the oval photo on the wall. Zinnia took my hand. "Let's go find Big Mama," she said.

All the way walking, she cried quietly. Some of my friends wanted me to play, but I pointed to Zinnia. They stared at her and walked with us for a while. When her friends ran up, they asked, "What's wrong with Zinnia?"

"Nothing," I said.

Soon they began to drift away. "Hey," I called, "if any of you see Mama Merryfield, take her home."

They all promised, and fanned out searching. Soon I heard whistling, and in the distance some boys beckoned. I ran toward them, dragging Zinnia.

The guys seemed pleased to have found Mama Merryfield, and I was glad I had asked for help. It would have taken us another hour because she was on a different street.

Mama Merryfield stood holding on to a light post. She looked sad, but she was humming "Nobody Knows the Trouble I Seen, Nobody Knows But Jesus."

I hugged her because she was our real mother. I suppose I had always saved a piece of my love for the phantom mother, but now I was free of any "holding back."

All three of us, hand in hand and swinging arms, walked home silently. The purple evening air felt like warm kisses on my face.

For dinner we had cornflakes and milk. There was a mushy banana apiece to cut over each bowl. The cool milk was creamy-sweet slipping down my throat, even though before Zinnia came home, I confess that I drank most of the cream off the top.

Zinnia was silent while we ate. After dinner she asked, "What about the rent money?"

She was asking me. My fifteen-year-old sister was asking twelve-year-old me about keeping that roof over our heads. I was flattered.

"We just need ten dollars?" I asked.

"Yes."

"I'll have it. And Zinnia," I said, "we got to stay awake. That money always disappears in the night."

She nodded and walked out front to talk to a girl-friend. I was amazed. She accepted my order to stay awake, and she hadn't asked how I would get the ten dollars.

But could I really earn that ten dollars from Officer Newton? Was my conclusion right? I needed time. If only I could zip across Montgomery on a bus. But, walking gave me thinking time.

I bathed at the faucet next door and went to bed.

Was I sure we only needed ten dollars? We had three days, two days the next morning. Zinnia still hadn't come in, but Big Mama was snoring.

I slipped from bed and pulled out my flashlight. The rent money in the red onion bag was still in place between laths of the wall. Zinnia had put paper strips on top of the bag so that anyone who moved it would spread shredded paper. My wet ink idea was good, but I didn't have any ink. After counting, I found we were short eight dollars and fifty-two cents, counting every penny. Ten dollars would cover perfectly.

Paper strips went back on top of the bag. Maybe this time we'd be safe. I stared at our hidden money. Suppose it did disappear? As a scientist I knew there had to be a reason. Nothing happened by magic.

A trap would be good. I put a big biology book, a cereal bowl, and two spoons by the money. Anyone touching the wall would make the book fall and hit my cereal bowl and two spoons.

I'd never sleep through all that clatter.

In the night, someone shook me. I had been dreaming of a string to trip the thief. When I sat up, Zinnia whispered, "Come listen."

We passed Mama Merryfield's bed. She was gone. Squeezing Zinnia's hand, I ran back for my flashlight, then followed her. As we ran to the end of the street, I heard Big Mama's voice in the bushes. She was crying.

"No, no, I don't have any money," she was saying.

By the light of the moon I saw that a man and a woman held her between them. I was ready to charge into them, but Zinnia held me back. She was right. We should find out what this was all about first.

A strange woman's voice said, "If you love them children like y'all say y'all do, y'all better get me what we asking for."

"True to the Lord," said Big Mama, "I don't have nothing for you. Go away."

"Old woman, y'all losing your mind," the woman said. "Y'all don't even know where y'all money be hid."

"She so old," said the man, "she ain't fit to raise them children. Y'all should tell the caseworkers to put them in a home and send her to the poorhouse."

The woman laughed, then coughed. For a moment she stepped into a stream of light. She wore a tight, dark dress and high heels. A cigarette glowed in her hand.

The smell was of those cigarettes called "reefers."

Some musicians at Zinnia's Saturday night dances smoked them during intermission. People said reefers made you silly in the head.

"I got my mind," Big Mama told them. "And y'all hurting my arm."

"That ain't all that's gonna be hurting you, old woman," the man said. It took all of Zinnia's strength to keep me from leaping at him.

I didn't know who these people were, but no one should treat Mama Merryfield like that. Right then I wasn't thinking about nonviolence. I wanted to fight. I wanted to kill those people.

The man was shorter than the strange woman, and wore loose pants and a glittery chain to his pants pocket. His hair was slicked back.

Zinnia dragged me behind a tree. Mosquitoes swarmed, stinging my arms and legs and neck. I slapped at them.

"They're the ones who take our rent money," whispered Zinnia.

I straightened up, surprised. "How do they know where to look? Why don't we hear them?"

"No, fool," said Zinnia. "Big Mama gives them our money."

That "fool" made me angry, I jerked from Zinnia and held my arm across my chest. Darkness seemed to close my throat.

Now Mama Merryfield's voice rang out: "Child, you used to make trips to Sundown for the social workers. Till you lost your job. You liked helping folks before you went crazy on them drugs. Listen to me. That's our rent money due soon."

The man shoved her. "Go get me twenty dollars, old woman, or she gonna take them children from you. She know who to tell."

When she heard that, Zinnia shook my shoulder and whispered, "What's your plan, Alfa?"

CHAPTER EIGHTEEN

Why did I have to have a plan? Zinnia sounded like Mr. Greendale. But, as usual, my sister was right. This blackmailing must have been going on for over a year. That's how long we had noticed money missing. Because these people had been stealing from us, we had to settle this once and for all.

I had to "put up my dukes." Defend all of us, but not by fighting. If nonviolence had worked with the three white boys, why not with these people?

Backing up, I bumped into a tree trunk. The tree felt good against my back. But I saw that the woman was dragging Big Mama toward our house.

"Oh, Lord, you're hurting me," said Big Mama with a whimper.

"Just get us twenty dollars, old woman, and y'all won't be hurting no more," said the man.

"Two days until the rent money due," Big Mama said. "I just gave you ten dollars the other day. I can't take the roof out from under the children's heads."

"Two days," the man said. "Y'all strong. You can work up a sweat and get you some twenty dollars."

After they passed a house, I heard a neighbor open his door. The man and woman with Big Mama began whispering. Hidden in shadows, Zinnia and I followed, listening. We crouched behind a hedge of holly bushes, then behind crepe myrtle trees along the street.

"Just twenty dollars?" asked Big Mama.

"That's right," the woman said in a voice like syrup. "Now don't y'all hurt her, Jake. She gonna get us the money."

"Get you the money," repeated Mama Merryfield. Her mind seemed to have slipped. So this was how it happened.

A plan. I jerked Zinnia's arm. "Let's love them," I said.

She hit me. "Are you crazy? We should kick their rears."

I shook my head. "No, no. Let's try it. Tell them we love them. Say we need them to get us scholarships, send us through high school and college. Send me to medical school."

Zinnia stood still. The man, woman, and Mama Merryfield walked farther ahead of us. Zinnia was thinking.

"Hug the woman and man," I whispered. I knew it sounded crazy. "Just overcome them with love." I heard another neighbor at a window. Did they know that these people were blackmailing our family? The neighbors must have seen these people with Big Mama before.

How was it I never woke up? I suppose we were usually too tired, Zinnia and me. We must have slept through these hoodlums visiting. I was glad Zinnia had stayed awake, since I'd forgotten to. Now we would speak to these people in "the manner of love."

I whispered, "Tell them we love them. Ask them for money." I was thinking that I'd call the man Mr. Jake, call the woman Mrs. Jake. In spite of my feelings, I'd treat them with respect. That was my plan; did Zinnia agree?

She took the flashlight from me. That was good. She'd show them what we looked like. Zinnia was thinking. She would begin. I heard her take a big breath.

A brain-numbing scream tore through the night air. "Well, lookee, Alfa," Zinnia called, loud enough to wake the dead. "It's our visitors of the night. We love you, we love you."

Jumping up and down, she hugged the woman. She knocked the reefer from her hand and swung her in a circle. Now all the neighbors were awake. Zinnia kept the flashlight on the man's and the woman's faces, not ours. I hadn't planned it like that.

"Lady, lady, ma'am," I called softly. "Mister, mister, sir. We love you both. We need you for money."

As Zinnia screamed louder, I called a little stronger. When Zinnia let go of the woman, I grabbed her bony body and swung her around. Zinnia was wrestling the man—and winning.

"Now we got money," she called, "our visitors are here to feed us and dress us . . ."

"And send us to college," I shouted. I could yell, too. I heard snickering. Out of the corner of my eye, I saw Big Mama sitting on the board to our house with her feet in the ditch water. She was laughing behind her hand.

"Medical school after college," I yelled even louder. Our neighbors began flicking their porch lights on. The woman's face looked terrified. So, she was afraid of being caught.

"She gonna love to support us, won't she, Alfa?"

"Yeah, Zinnia. Now we got our night visitor, Mrs. Jake, ma'am." I swung her around again. Zinnia kept the flashlight lighting the woman's face. I let go of her and ran to Mr. Jake.

I hugged him, holding his arms down. He was pretty weak for a man, but I felt a knife in his pocket. It was on a chain. He shouted, "Get away from me. Y'all crazy. These kids crazy."

"We love you, we love you," I sang. Zinnia joined me. "We love you, we love you. Now y'all can take care of us. We love y'all." We were chanting at the tops of our voices.

First the two of us jerked the man around, then we

jerked the woman around. We shoved them back to back, and started jumping up and down around them. Zinnia swung the flashlight back and forth across their eyes. I began a chant: "Money, money, money, give us money, money, money."

Zinnia joined me. "Money, money, money!"

The woman finally caught her breath. "Get away. I don't want anything to do with y'all. If Mama Merryfield don't give us money, I'm gonna send y'all to a home."

"A home, a home," Zinnia shouted. "Our night visitors gonna get us a home. We gonna have a home, home, home."

"Yeah," I said softer. And I kept an eye on that knife in the man's pocket. I was glad we weren't fighting them. Yet, the condition they were in, these people didn't have any power.

"Maybe she want us to live with her, huh, Alfa?"

"Yeah," I called, joining Zinnia jumping around the two. "They gonna give us money, money, money. Send us to school, school, school."

I twirled the woman again, hugged her, and jumped up and down. She was weak, too, nothing but skin and bones. I could swing her like an armful of straw.

The man wasn't much heavier, and his arms in long shirt sleeves were like sticks—no muscles. At twelve I was taller than either of them, and more muscular. Their breaths stank of cigarettes and some kind of alcoholic drink. Their clothes and skins smelled sour.

The man began running from us. Zinnia chased him.

"Mister, mister," I called. "Don't go. We love you so."

I grabbed the woman and spun her. "I love you, I love you."

"Let go of me. Y'all crazy," said the woman, holding her head. She seemed dizzy after being swung around and having the light flash in her eyes. "I don't want nothing to do with y'all. I ain't never coming here again."

"Money, money, money," I called. "You got to send me to college and medical school."

"No, no, get away from me." I twirled her a last time, but she was reaching for the man. She tried to run after him.

"But we both love you," said Zinnia, returning from chasing the man. She caught the woman's dress, and it tore. As the woman ran, she broke the heel off her shoe. Picking it up, she ran limping down the street after the man.

I stood watching them, and I felt furious. Imagine! Mama Merryfield had tried to keep us by giving them money. Paying them off, and they were sick from drink and drugs. The woman might have been an aide to social workers once, but she was helpless now. As they disappeared in the darkness, our neighbors clapped from their front porches.

I helped Mama Merryfield get to her feet, and the three of us went in to bed. As I closed my eyes that night, I heard Big Mama saying, "Lord, Lord, what was

I thinking? What was wrong with me?" I had a feeling that was the nonviolent end of the night visitors, but I still had to worry about the rent.

I wondered: Will I really earn that rent money from Officer Newton tomorrow?

CHAPTER NINETEEN

The next day at Greendale Grocery, I raced around getting shelves stocked and produce put in place. I mean, I ran around in that store like a cat with a mousetrap on his tail. When I glanced up, I saw Mr. Greendale leaning in the doorway with his arms folded. He was staring at me.

I wiped my hands on the white apron I wore. I supposed that he was admiring how fast and well I worked. Already I had emptied his produce from the truck outside, and stocked all the shelves. I walked over to him.

"Sir," I said, "Officer Newton wants to see me at noon today. But I have to run some errands first." I cleared my throat. "I'll be back in about two hours, sir. May I have the time off, sir?"

It occurred to me that using the bus would have cut those two hours into about forty-five minutes. I kept dimes in my pocket.

"Get out," said Mr. Greendale.

"Sir?"

"Get out and stay out. You're fired, Alfa Merryfield."

I stood with my mouth open. That was so unexpected that tears spurted into my eyes.

"You heard me," Mr. Greendale said. "I'm a businessman in this community, and I've been thinking. Ain't no criminal Nigra gonna work for me."

A criminal? I wasn't a criminal. And this job was not only five dollars every two weeks, but food for our family. Now we'd be back to picking from garbage Dumpsters.

I took off my apron, threw it on a peg in the storage room, and walked out the back door. I was more disgusted than angry. Somehow I had thought Mr. Greendale was different. That he'd been on my side. But I was wrong.

Now my family would be hungry.

Outside, Alabama sunshine blasted my back with heat. I stood wondering. Did Mr. Greendale want me to beg for my job? I thought about his look, his words: "Get out and stay out. You're fired."

He had sounded final and angry. I was shocked, but I had work to do. I had needed time; now I had time.

In the next block a public library crowned the corner. The two-story building had an arched doorway. From my school's book corner I knew inside there would be a card file to look up "social security." Why didn't I use this time?

I walked up the stone steps boldly. Officer Newton had told me it was all right. The card file was in the first well-lit room. I found the "S" drawer.

Suddenly a guard ran up and struck my shoulder with a stick. "What're y'all stealing, boy?"

I felt guilty. I wondered if he knew about the bicycle. "Sir?"

"Where's the book?"

I raised my arms. "I haven't got any book, sir. I was looking it up first."

"You must've stolen something." He blew a whistle. Another guard ran up and struck me on the head.

"What're you doing in here, nigger?" asked the second guard.

My head was ringing. "Officer Newton sent me, sir."

"Liar!" They both struck my back. "He'd never send you here."

I held my arms over my head and crouched. I wanted to scream and hit back, but I knew that wouldn't work.

"He did, sir."

"I'll call him." A phone sat on a desk near the wall. The first guard started to lift the receiver. He held his hand on it and looked at me.

I nodded. "He did, sir."

The other guard struck my legs. It hurt so much, I moaned. "I'm calling him."

Slowly, I stood up and lowered my arms. But when the second guard moved, I jumped and held my head with both arms again. He said, "Don't y'all never come to this library again, boy!"

The guard nodded. "Jimmy," said the first guard, "this is your cousin, Sam. We got a nigger boy here who says you sent him to this public library." He turned to me. "What's your name?"

"Alfa Merryfield, sir." I tried to stand tall again.

"That's the one," he told Officer Newton. "Oh, yeah, old Aunt Lydia? Sure. I know her. All right, Jimmy, and thank you." He hung up the phone. "We can let him go, Tom," he said. "Seems there was a little misunderstanding. Y'all don't have to do nothing now, boy. Jimmy will handle things with the State."

What state? My head was still ringing, and my leg felt torn in two. The library guards patted my back. One offered me a paper cup of "white" water from their fountain.

Shaking my head no to their water, I limped out of that public library. I felt ashamed of my mistake. It was dumb to go to a library before checking with someone colored first. There were probably books somewhere else for us.

However, my main job was earning that ten dollars for the rent. Stop thinking about Mr. Greendale or the library, I told myself, and I turned off my mind.

As I limped uphill in the morning heat, I thought about the missing money. I wished Zinnia were with me. Alone, I went over what I knew.

Mama Merryfield, Zinnia, and I were present at the yellow house, along with Mrs. Louise Cook. Mrs. Cook said Paul Adams was Mrs. Williams's brother, and sometimes hung out at Dr. Williams's house. I hadn't seen Paul Adams that morning. He did have money enough to leave his job, however. I didn't know how he got the money.

Dr. Williams had returned for his money. He may have owed it to Mr. Plumber, the local loan shark. Mrs. Williams had missed the money, and had called the police. The policeman was Officer Newton. Big Mama found a handbill for a pawnshop at Mrs. Williams's house. I saw the silver money clip in that same pawnshop window.

What else? The money clip had disappeared from the shop window, and Dr. Williams hadn't been pleased to hear where his silver clip was.

As I walked, I looked around. For a few moments I stood under a magnolia tree with some blooms still fragrant. Because I could see the redbrick Union Station, I knew I was near Tallapoosa and Commerce Streets. Moving faster, I trotted down the tunnel under the railroad. That tunnel led to one of my favorite places, a spot where I could touch the waters of our Alabama River. Flowing waters always soothed me.

Mama Merryfield said that years ago, wagons used to roll down the tunnel carrying bales of cotton to boats headed for Mobile, and from Mobile to England. Now it's like a park. The river was warm and sparkling in sunlight, but what I saw made me feel even more disturbed.

Behind some trash cans I spied a man sleeping. He was hugging his shoes and a paper bag of clothes.

Homeless. Without my job we had less money for the rent.

We Merryfields could become homeless. Of course, the neighbors and church people would pass us around from house to house for a while. They had helped another family like that. But those people soon disappeared. Some said they traveled to Mississippi. Others said they went into the woods and died.

Never before had I let myself think about what would happen if we were homeless. I shivered in the heat and glanced in a trash can. After a quick look around, I pulled out a half-eaten banana. I spit out the first bite and ate the rest. Tears rolled again as I left the river and walked the downtown.

I had to stare in a store window so people wouldn't notice that I was crying. How unfair could life be? Why was I trying so hard to be 'somebody?'

Dr. Alfa Merryfield. What a "dumb dream!"

A clock in a store window showed nine-thirty. I had a job to do before noon. Wiping sweat off my face, I limped with purpose. Couldn't look suspicious hanging around downtown.

When I passed Zinnia's dry-cleaning store, I walked to the back and tapped on her window. She saw me and ran out.

"What?" she asked.

"Lost my job."

"Why?"

"Asked for time."

"Can't get it back?"

I shook my head. "Fired."

"He'll be sorry," she said, and tapped my shoulder. "I'll come straight home."

"No food," I said.

"Oh, no!" She hugged me, and both of us cried.

Finally I pushed her toward the door. "Keep your job," I said.

She nodded and walked back in. What a great sister I had. And Mama Merryfield—we still had each other. I hadn't told Zinnia I'd gotten beaten at the library.

As I limped along the street, I heard a group of white kids coming. I slowed down and stepped off the sidewalk for them, but they joined me walking in the street. I dared not look at their faces, but I heard a girl's voice.

"We all walking, too," she said softly with a nervous kind of giggle. "We don't ride the bus."

I walked faster, but they walked faster, too. Was trouble chasing me?

"What's y'all name?" an older voice asked.

Clearing my throat, I said, "Alfred, sir."

"I'm Turner."

"And Nancy."

"And Donald." Donald sounded young.

"And we all walk everywhere now," the girl, Nancy, said.

When I slowed down, they walked slower. When I speeded up, they stepped up faster. A bus passed us.

By now, the white kids kind of made me angry. I said in a loud voice, "I'm walking until they treat my sister and Big Mama right."

"We all walking till they treat y'all folks decent, too," said the older boy. "Bye, Alfred."

They turned onto a side street, and I had a chance to look at them. The plump, dark-haired girl was maybe Zinnia's age; the light-haired, tall boy might have been eighteen; and the small, dark-haired, little boy might have been about eight years old. They weren't laughing at me or anything. They were just walking. The girl turned and waved. I was too surprised to wave back.

At first I didn't know what to think, then I felt pleased.

In an hour's walk from the dry cleaners, I was at the yellow house. What excuse would I give for walking to the back door or even up the drive?

My head hurt so bad, I sat on the curb in the shade of a crepe myrtle tree. I was still hungry. Soon I heard footsteps. Mrs. Louise Cook trotted along the drive with a heavy paper bag. "I thought that be y'all, Alfa. I wanted to give this to someone deserving."

"Yes, ma'am."

"Here's a ham and fresh collards." Why was she giving me food? Was she buying me off?

"Oh, thank you, ma'am." Through two greasy bags and newspaper wrapping I could smell that warm ham. It was heavy, too, a full ham. "Is this all right to take, ma'am?"

"They owe you more than that. Today be my last day here," she said in a low voice. "I'm leaving now."

"Oh, ma'am. Were you fired?"

"No. I quit. Ain't been paid lately, and I be sick and tired of her treating me rotten."

"Yes, ma'am."

"Spends more time on her plants than on her people. Why, this week she bought some kind o' green fruit tree for the side yard. The tree nursery man said this be no weather for tree planting, but she insisted. She make a man water it day and night."

"Yes, ma'am."

"That woman also got herself a dwarf banana plant for the front porch, and more of them orchid flowering plants."

"Yes, ma'am."

"Besides," Mrs. Cook said in an even lower voice, "my husband and me got relatives in Birmingham. Tonight we gonna go live down there. My husband gonna find him a new job there."

"Yes, ma'am." They were leaving Montgomery, and he didn't even have a job?

I stood up. Now I had all the evidence I needed. My hypothesis met the test. We would never work at that yellow house again, and I had to walk that heavy ham all the way home. And then I'd walk back to meet Officer Newton.

CHAPTER TWENTY

I returned to the police station for the noon meeting. This time we met in a small, air-conditioned room across from Officer Newton's desk. A red geranium bloomed on the windowsill, and the drone of the air conditioner sounded like a dozen bees.

"So y'all think y'all know who stole Dr. Williams's money?" Officer Newton said.

All the way back to town I had worked out how to tell him. Of course, I could mention all the people who didn't steal the money. Suspects: Mama Merryfield, Zinnia, Alfa, Dr. Williams, Mr. Plumber, Mrs. Louise Cook, Mr. Paul Adams.

I could tell how we thought Dr. Williams had put Mrs. Cook up to taking it and returning it to him. Or how we thought Mr. Paul Adams came through and stole it. But that would be mixing the apples and the oranges.

True, I had mixed the lemons and limes once, and it looked fine, but I didn't want to confuse Officer Newton.

I decided to speak directly to the point. "Sir," I said, holding my head, "I believe Mrs. Williams stole her husband's money. She gave some of it to her brother, Paul Adams, and spent the rest. She doesn't get much spending money, not even enough to pay her help. And she loves expensive plants. This week she had a new tree planted on her hillside, and she bought a dwarf banana tree and orchids for the porch."

Officer Newton flipped his notebook closed. "Then I don't have a case, do I?"

"Yes, sir, you do," I said, nodding my head. "We're all still accused of stealing, sir, and Dr. Williams doesn't know."

"He knows," said Officer Newton. "He's been trying to get me to terminate the case. I suspect the pawnshop attendant described his wife as the person pawning his silver money clip."

"Oh," I said.

"And we wouldn't want to embarrass a fine, Southern lady like Mrs. Williams, now would we, Alfa?"

What the policeman had left out was the word "WHITE." He didn't want to embarrass a fine Southern WHITE lady. But he didn't mind embarrassing my fine Southern COLORED great-grandmother. I could have spit in his eye.

"Sir," I said. "How about our pay?" That was justice.

"Well, Alfa," Officer Newton said, "we both know y'all won't be getting paid. However, after cousin Sam and Tom called from the library, I checked into that social security. Aunt Lydia should be getting a monthly social security check beginning this July." He smiled.

"I applied for it by phone. She's been due it for years. All she needs to do is sign the form when it comes. She'll get a big check for the six months of this year that she missed."

Social security? It was for colored people, too? That would be a big help. What else? How about my job?

"Sir," I said, sliding forward on the chair. "Mr. Greendale fired me this morning. He feels I'm a criminal or something because you came to the store for me. I would be grateful if you could speak to him, sir."

He nodded. "I'll do that." He pulled out a file and tore it in half, then each half in half. "Y'all are no longer accused of burglary, Alfa."

Sure, fine. He could tear up the police report. But would that ease our past eight days of misery?

I slid to the edge of the seat.

"Oh, yes," he said. He reached in his pocket and handed me a crisp ten-dollar bill.

I stared at the money, and for some reason I didn't say thank you. When I left him, I didn't look back. I hoped he would remember to call Mr. Greendale, and I wished he would stop the white boys if they were ever beating me again.

Tripping and hobbling on my sore knee and my sore legs. I ran uphill and down on the way home. I waved at the drivers of those almost empty buses. Smiled in the windows of the downtown stores, likewise almost empty, and I wasn't sorry for the owners. They never treated us right.

At home that evening I sat in the front doorway waiting for Big Mama and Zinnia. Our baked ham smelled wonderful. I had used some of it to season the collard greens while they cooked, and I had cooked rice, too. We had a feast awaiting us.

Zinnia strolled up with three girlfriends. She turned at the ditch and said good-bye so they wouldn't follow her. "I have to talk to my brother," she told them.

They glared at me.

"Smells good," she said.

"Ham."

"Who?"

"Mrs. Louise Cook."

"Why?"

"Leaving town."

"Guilty?"

"No."

"Who?"

"Mrs. Williams."

"Paul Adams?"

"Mrs. Williams gave."

"Dr. Williams?"

"Knows."

"How?"

"Pawnshop."

She shrugged. "Police know?"

"Tore up report."

"Rent money?"

I handed her the ten-dollar bill from my pocket.

"Wow." She grinned. Later I would tell her the details, maybe even tell her about the library. But for now it was nice to sit side by side in silence.

"Big Mama." Zinnia pointed as a car cruised down our street. I was pleased and stood up.

"Thank you for giving her a ride, sir," I told the man.

Zinnia took Big Mama's arm. She walked her toward the house, and the man drove off.

As I strolled behind them, I thought the medical degree of Dr. Alfa Merryfield had gone in one day from "dumb dream" to "dramatic possibility."

Just then Mr. Greendale, a silly, sorry grin on his face, drove up in his rusty, old truck. My job and food are back, I thought. Turning, I strolled to meet him. I couldn't help smiling.

I seemed to hear our red Alabama dirt cry out, "Truth pressed down to earth, will rise again. Not victory, but justice." Way to go! I thought.

AUTHOR'S NOTE

More than any book of historical fiction I've written to date, this story stirred my emotions. I lived under segregation.

On my bicycle, as a child in Virginia, I tried to race in the rain through a "white neighborhood" to reach home. Using this route, I would be home (the next street over) in one block, using the long way around, I would have had to ride several blocks. But black children weren't allowed in white neighborhoods.

In spite of the rain, white people screamed at me from their porches, and one gentleman got in his car and tried to run me down. His neighbors clapped. I was about ten years old.

I remember not only sitting in the back of the bus

but, as a teen, being put off the bus for not noticing that a white person needed my seat.

In Louisiana I sat behind the screen that read COLORED. If more white people boarded the bus, I had to get up and carry that screen farther to the rear of the bus. At that time I was teaching biology courses at Xavier University, in New Orleans.

Most painful of all, in Washington, D.C., public libraries, I was followed, questioned, and harassed. As a child I begged for a library card, but I never felt welcomed.

As a teacher I could walk into the library in New Orleans, but I couldn't "loiter" looking up books. I couldn't sit or stand. Rough guards with sticks ordered me to "keep moving."

These humiliations have never left me. In new places, I feel "instant replays" of racial fears. Occasionally I suffer a moment of panic as I enter a library, and I practically live in libraries for research.

Montgomery, Alabama, has no community called Sundown. The Merryfield family is also fictional. But I hope I have captured what actual people in Montgomery said "walking" meant for them. I have talked to them, and have read oral histories of those days.

I know what civil rights demonstrations meant for me. For a few years our family joined in vigils, in testing of realtors, and in weekly marches for fair housing. We had the privilege of marching in Chicago with Dr. Martin Luther King, Jr. Taking part in that nonviolent struggle established my self-respect as an African-American.

In 1956, when this story is set, people of color could not go to schools, movie theaters, restaurants, motels, hotels, or public bathrooms; they could not drink from water fountains or ride on buses and trains—except in segregated ways.

Voting was "discouraged" by injury and loss of jobs.

African-Americans paid the same money as white people for clothes in stores but, unlike white people, they could not try on the clothes for proper fit, or return them.

Bus segregation was humiliating everywhere in the South, but it was outstandingly embarrassing in Montgomery, Alabama. Not only did people of color have to sit in the rear, and give up their seats when whites needed them, but they had to pay in the front, and then get off and run to board the bus by a rear door.

However, determination to change the System was growing among African-Americans. In the 1940s blacks could fight for freedom for others in the Second World War, but they returned to segregation for themselves in America—"land of the free."

In 1954 the Supreme Court declared segregated schools unconstitutional. Hopes rose. In August 1955 fourteen-year-old Emmett Till died a brutal death for "misspeaking" to a white woman. Deaths like his were no longer acceptable.

The time for a change in the System was at hand. When Mrs. Rosa Parks, a highly respected woman in Montgomery, was arrested for not giving up her seat to a white man, the black community took action. After all, more than 75 percent of the riders on Montgomery buses were black.

The Women's Political Council, organized ten years before, phoned black citizens. The women decided on a one-day bus boycott. Ms. Jo Ann Robinson, English professor at all-black Alabama State College, ran off handbills announcing the boycott. Students spread out over the city carrying the notices to people in Montgomery and surrounding areas.

Mr. E. D. Nixon bailed Mrs. Rosa Parks out of jail and called the Reverend Ralph Abernathy. The twenty-nine-year-old Reverend Abernathy helped organize the black ministers. At the first church meeting, five thousand people were inside Holt Street Baptist Church, and loudspeakers reached thousands outside who could not get in.

Later, when the Montgomery Improvement Association (MIA) was formed, they chose the twenty-six-year-old Reverend Martin Luther King, Jr., as president. This newcomer was a first-year minister at Dexter Avenue Baptist Church, in downtown Montgomery, and a graduate student for a Ph.D. in theology from Boston University.

Nonviolence was the highly Christian weapon that the Reverend King preached. It had worked for Gandhi in India's struggle for freedom. The one-day bus boycott continued indefinitely.

Negotiations failed. The City Commissioners and the bus company refused to agree to mild requests: first-come, first-serve seating for blacks from the back and whites from the front; not having to give up a seat to a white person; and having black drivers on some routes.

Next, black lawyers took their case to the federal district court, and then to the Supreme Court. African-Americans won in both courts.

After about thirteen months (381 days) of walking, African-Americans like Alfa Merryfield and his family boarded the Montgomery buses, free to sit where they wished.

Their success set off nonviolent demonstrations to integrate restaurants, buses, trains, and waiting rooms all over the United States. Young people joined the demonstrations and went to jail for justice.

Some white people united with blacks in the struggle. "Black and white together, we shall overcome," they sang. Voter registration grew in the South in spite of fear and punishment. Black students applied to high schools, colleges, and universities that had formerly been all white.

Today, Montgomery, Alabama, is welcoming and friendly. My husband and I visited there in the last week of June 1997 to research this story. Strangers, black and white, ended every conversation with: "Montgomery has changed, you know."

We stood by the flowing waters of the beautiful Civil Rights Memorial in Montgomery. Its circular-table fountain gives a chronicle of events, and a list of forty people who gave their lives in the struggle. On a rectangular-wall fountain we read these words: UNTIL JUSTICE ROLLS DOWN LIKE WATERS, AND RIGHTEOUSNESS LIKE A MIGHTY STREAM.

Segregation has been outlawed. However, housing and schools in many places remain segregated, and jobs for blacks are often limited. The struggle goes on.

Look around you. Don't feel left out. Listen to the news. Young people of today have important roles to play in working for justice.

BIBLIOGRAPHY

Hampton, Henry, and Steve Fayer. *Voices of Freedom: An Oral History of the Civil Rights Movement from the 1950s through the 1980s.* New York: Bantam Books, 1990.

King, Martin Luther, Jr. *Stride Toward Freedom: The Montgomery Story.* New York: Harper & Row, 1958.

King, Martin Luther, Jr. *The Words of Martin Luther King, Jr.* Selected by Coretta Scott King. New York: Newmarket Press, 1987.

Powledge, Fred. *Free At Last? The Civil Rights Movement and the People Who Made It.* Boston: Little, Brown, and Company, 1991.

Williams, Juan. *Eyes on the Prize: America's Civil Rights Years 1954-1965.* New York: Viking Penguin Inc., 1987.